CAPTIVE BRIDE

THE SECRET BRIDE SERIES

ALTA HENSLEY

Special Thank you to my editor: Maggie Ryan and my wonderful beta readers.

Cover Design: Jay Aheer

DEDICATION

To my family who understand just what it takes to finish a book.

1

THERE'S A FLY IN THE HONEY.

The contamination must be rid.

Please allow him to be the one who gets away.

"Run. Run," I whisper against the glass of the window. My breath fogs my vision, but I can still see. "It's not too late. You still have time. Run."

He can't hear me. They never hear me.

I consider pounding my fists against the glass to capture his attention but know that will only make it worse. If he sees me... he'll continue to come forward in curiosity. He won't run away.

He *needs* to run away. He just doesn't know it yet.

There's a fly in the honey and Hell will be paid.

He's not the first. He won't be the last.

Please, please, please allow this man to be the one who gets away.

My heart stops as he points his camera in my direction. What if he sees me? What if I'm in his picture? Will I be to blame for what comes next? I know what's in store. It's always the same.

Although there is something different in this man from the others. His camera looks bigger and harder to use. He has to spin the front of it back and forth as he takes the pictures. He's dressed differently than the ones before him. Hiking boots, khaki pants with lots of pockets, a cream cotton shirt that buttons with sleeves rolled to his upper arms above the elbows. His attire makes him appear more worldly than the others. Like he's on an adventure rather than just a sightseeing day trip.

Yes, he's different.

But he's still the fly in the honey and will have to face the consequences. There's nothing I can do. I know this.

He should have stayed on the beaten path. He should have heeded the warnings of the no trespassing signs. There is plenty to see down the hill. The old, abandoned buildings in the main part of Hallelujah Junction are just as good as the ones up here. The ghost town and main attraction are down the hill.

Not here.

There's an old church, a mercantile, pharmacy, a livery, and even a small jail. All the houses remain standing and preserved. Inside is the left behind furniture of the 1800s residents who built this mining town before they all vacated in a hurry for some unknown reason. History frozen in time. Secrets and whispers of the ghosts mesmerize people from around the world.

Why had the townsfolk left in such a hurry?

Why would they leave their belongings behind?

These were the eerie questions that made Hallelujah Junction become the tourist attraction that it was.

The tourists can see the schoolhouse from the main street. It towers on the top of Cemetery Road meant to look at but never approach. There are several buildings in Hallelujah Junction that are strictly off limits to the public due to safety reasons. The signs clearly mark the prohibited from the welcome.

So why? Why does he ignore the signs? There are just as many worn-down houses and dilapidated pieces of history to take pictures of in the main area. Stay with the tourists. Stay where it's safe. Listen to the ranger and follow the rules. The rules are simple: Stay on the paths. No littering. No destruction of property. *Stay. On. The. Paths.*

The rules are so simple.

Break the rules, and you will pay the price.

I see his shadow first. The ranger.

He has a job.

Enforce the rules.

I should leave the window and walk away. Pine Cone, my cat, rubs along my leg begging for some attention. She knows what is good for me. I should listen to her. I don't need to see this. I shouldn't see this. But I can never look away. This time could be different.

The man is larger than the ranger. His shoulders are broad and his chest wide. It appears as if he could run faster with his long, lean legs. He could resist and win. Maybe that is why he broke the rules. Maybe he knows he can.

But I don't want him to hurt the ranger.

The ranger is my Papa Rich. He's mine. He's all I have.

I hold my breath, not sure what I want to see. Whose side am I on? The rule breaker or my Papa Rich?

"You're trespassing," I hear Papa Rich say. The glass of the window is thin. The air is still.

The rule breaker turns, startled. "Oh sorry, man. I'll be out of your hair in just a second. I'm shooting an article for *Rolling Stone* called 'Find Your Wild.' I want to make sure I capture it all."

"Did you not see the signs?"

"I'll be quick. I saw the schoolhouse up here on the hill and needed to get a better picture up close." He continues taking pictures as if the ranger has no power over what he does or doesn't do.

Papa Rich's jaw tightens. His eyes narrow. I recognize this look. I know exactly what comes next. Papa Rich looks at the old schoolhouse. At me. I'm hidden away in the structure of this trespasser's dangerous obsession.

Can he see me? No. I know the way the sun is angled that the reflection protects me from the eyes of others. I know the times of the day I'm safe from view. Years and years have made me an expert. Papa Rich can't see me but no doubt knows I'm watching. He knows I can see. I can hear. I will learn from this man's mistakes. Another lesson of what happens to those who break the rules.

"The story of the ghost girl in the school

window is fascinating," the rule breaker says as he snaps away. "I want to make sure I really get the right images to go with it." He doesn't stop taking pictures. "Have you ever seen the ghost while working here? I'd really like to interview you if you have."

"There's no trespassing up here," Papa Rich repeats.

The rule breaker doesn't look away from the schoolhouse. He should. He really should.

Like so many times before, Papa Rich pulls a thick wooden mallet from his knapsack he carries every day and hits the rule breaker on the back of the head. The sickening crack echoes up the path and stabs at my heart.

Yes, the rule breaker is bigger. Yes, he could run faster. But just like the others, he falls to the ground. The lens of his fancy camera shatters on the desert dirt and scatters beneath the branches of the sagebrush.

I turn away from the window then and finally pet Pine Cone under her chin. I don't need to see what comes next. I know Papa Rich will drag his limp body to the acid pits in the old mill building.

Another tragic accident.

Another careless tourist who didn't pay attention to the danger signs and falls to his death in the pits. It's not like anyone will find the rule breaker. The acid pits will sizzle his flesh and bone until nothing is left.

The fly in the honey will be rectified. Contamination will be cleansed.

2

EMBER

I HATE THE SOUND OF THE DOOR OPENING AND shutting after a trespasser is dealt with. Papa Rich is always in such a foul mood. Without fail, he'll lecture me and cite the Bible as if I am the one who has committed the crime. I'll have no choice but to stare on with wide eyes, nodding on occasion, and give every visual cue I possibly can that I am receptive of his schooling and learning about the difference between good and evil.

Yes, Papa Rich.

You're right, Papa Rich.

He deserved to pay for his crimes, Papa Rich.

You're just acting as the hand of God, Papa Rich. I'll pray for his soul.

But the sounds coming from the front of the schoolhouse sound different. So different, that I consider hiding as I was taught to do if anyone other than Papa Rich were to ever enter the building.

"Ember," Papa Rich calls out. "Ember, get out here."

I pad barefoot against the cool wood floor cautiously. Something is wrong. Something is very wrong. I can feel it. I can hear it in the way he says my name, winded.

I peer around the wall and freeze in my tracks.

Papa Rich has hold of the rule breaker underneath his arms. He's dragging him inside the door.

No acid pits.

No discarding of the body as if it were trash.

The rule breaker lay limp, unconscious and is awkwardly being yanked with all the force Papa Rich can muster. The stranger's dusty from being dragged along the dirt path, and there's a matted patch of blood on the back of his head from where he was hit.

I can't tell if the man is alive or dead.

Am I supposed to be a hand of God today? I don't want to.

I swallow the bile down.

Papa Rich looks up, his blue eyes hold me frozen as he motions me towards him. His greasy hair sticks to his temples as sweat beads down his sun-weathered face.

I watch a small grin curl his lips as he says, "Give me a hand, Ember. Don't just stand there."

I can see the man is too big for Papa Rich. I'm guessing that is why Papa Rich didn't just drag him to the old mill himself. Maybe it was too far. But I don't want to go to the acid pits. I had been there before and begged Papa Rich to never make me do it again. He said if I was a good girl, I wouldn't have to. I was a good girl, but my heart stops in fear that Papa Rich blames me for this man crossing the trespassing line.

His nostrils flare, and the cords in his neck strain. I recognize his hardened emotions and am scared. "Pick up his feet. Help me carry him to the hatch."

His command ricochets through my body. Although having a direct order makes it easy for me to comply. I take hold of the man's ankles and lift while I stumble and shuffle my feet as Papa Rich walks backwards.

He directs his gaze to my shaking hands. "Don't drop him."

My lungs labor for air, and my muscles burn. The man is heavy, and I don't understand why we are taking him to the hatch, but I don't dare question Papa Rich. When he has a plan, we follow it.

I have never seen a dead body up close before

and having to touch one makes the taste of vomit linger in the back of my throat.

When we finally reach the hatch, Papa Rich says, "Put him down and rest for a moment."

The thud of the body hitting the dusty schoolroom floor strikes me with a reality I'm not sure I can face.

Papa slides the antique school desk that conceals the hatch across the planked floor. It's our secret. Only ours. The hatch opens to an underground tunnel that connects to other tunnels running beneath all the buildings in Hallelujah Junction. The miners of yesteryear built the tunnels, and Papa Rich made them safer by reinforcing and adding battery-operated lighting. It's how we walk among the tourists undetected. *Like mice*, Papa Rich used to tell me. I never leave the buildings. I never go outside. I only use the tunnels. It's the rule.

I don't move. My gaze is paralyzed on the man's face. I take in the straight profile of his nose, the sharp angle of his jaw, and the wayward brown hairs on his head in desperate need of a trim.

"We need to bring him to the house." Papa's order is sharp and unkind.

A tremor shivers through my heart. My pulse thrashes in my throat. I open my mouth to refuse, but the hard look in Papa's eye changes my mind.

He opens the hatch, silently motions for me to

pick up the man's feet again, and I obey. I scan the room for Pine Cone hoping she is near and won't somehow get out of the schoolhouse. Papa Rich had warned me time and time again that there are vicious wild animals outside that would tear her flesh to bits, and I was to never open the doors or the windows if I valued her life. I would normally carry her through the tunnels but know that is not a possibility right now. I will have to come back for her later.

As we awkwardly push the body down the hatch and stand in the base of the tunnel, Papa Rich twists around, scrutinizing the distance of our journey. "Come on. Let's get going before he comes to."

Comes to?

Is he alive?

Not dead?

My stomach cramps, and my heartbeat slams into a rapid staccato at this new piece of information. If he is alive, why are we taking him to our home? We never have guests... well, not really. Papa Rich has a friend named Scarecrow who comes to visit often, but I don't consider him a guest. He's not wanted by me. I wish he never comes, and whenever he does, he leaves a stench of onion and sweat that takes days to rid.

Releasing a heavy breath, I do as Papa Rich says and hurry down the tunnel as fast as I physically can. I bite down on my lip to not cry out as my bare feet scrape against the cold and jagged rocks. I don't have the time to take careful steps as I usually do.

"Come on, we're almost there. Good girl. You're doing so good," he praises as he huffs and puffs with the weight of the unconscious man in his arms.

Tears blur my vision as I stare at the man, hating myself for my part in whatever this is. I don't know why we are doing this. I don't know Papa Rich's plan and how any of this could possibly be a good idea. But I know deep down to the tip of my now bloody toes that something is wrong.

When we finally reach the hatch leading to the main house Papa Rich and I live in, I somehow find the words to say, "Papa Rich, what are we doing?"

When his eyes meet mine, the sinister secret only he knows looms near. A surge of terror scorches through my veins.

"There's a serpent in the garden," he says. "Judas among us." He begins to pull the man up the hatch to our home. "So blood will be shed. Unless... unless..."

I exhale a chest full of air as I do my part in this misdeed. I know it is wrong. My Papa Rich is supposed to be a Godly man. A man I never question. But my soul screams no. No, no, no.

Forgive me, God. What do I do? Forgive me, God. Forgive me.

With one final push, the man—the stranger— is now in our home.

Hello, Devil. Nice to meet you.

3

RICHARD

Twenty Years Ago

If a town could be the hairy armpit of the devil, this town would be it. I roll up the cracked window of my pick-up truck to prevent inhaling the fetor of poverty and white trash. If it were possible to avoid this town completely, I would. I hate it. I hate it. I hate it. But I need supplies. As soon as I get them bought and loaded in the back of my truck, I will hightail it back to Hallelujah Junction and not leave again until I have to do another supply run.

Hallelujah Junction... my salvation.

God blessed me the day he found me the job of being a ranger for the infamous ghost town hidden in the hills of Nevada. An old mining town long abandoned by the residents for an unknown reason. The 1800s town's current popularity centers around the fact that every ancient resident left with only the clothes on their backs and what little supplies they could carry. They left everything behind in a hurry to flee. All the furniture, dishes, books, handcrafted items, family heirlooms, hand-stitched clothing, and the hidden secrets of why they deserted their homes remained. It makes the haunted town a living museum of a time long ago. An eerie place turned to stone as if touched by Medusa. Tourists would come from all over the world to see history paused. They wanted answers. Why? Why would the people build a life here, and then vacate so quickly without taking what meant everything to them and what they had worked so hard to gain? Reasons were rumors and speculations only. Plague? Dangers from the daily mining and plundering of the earth such as poisoned water or toxic gases? Impending attack from nearby Indian tribes? No one knew.

I don't care why they left. I'm happy they did. The town is mine. They left me a gift. Yes, I have to share the bottom half of my utopia with the common folk, even though I despise each one of them. But regardless, Hallelujah Junction is my paradise before I reach Kingdom Come.

But the truth remains...

They stink.

An odor of money and materialism.

A redolence of false promises and fake smiles.

They are walking misery cloaked in designer clothes and shoes.

I loathe the air around them.

But I have a job to perform if I want to remain in my paradise. I have to watch over them and enforce the rules that my boss handed me in a weathered pamphlet when he offered me the position. Health codes, environmental mandates, dictates from the government and all the laws I have to not only abide by but guarantee are followed perfectly.

But the upper half of the town is where I live. I was given a house so that I can live on-site. It is the only piece of property that had been outfitted to meet modern day needs. I would have gladly accepted one of the historical houses and live off the grid, but I was handed the ranger's house that has indoor plumbing and electricity. Being a ranger is comfortable, and it pays well—not that I have any real need for paper money other than my monthly run into town for supplies. My wealth comes from the land and my solitude.

And the tourists only come during the warmer weather months. The winter brings snow so severe that the dirt road leading up to Hallelujah Junction is often closed down until the melt. I plan for those months and stockpile my goods. I look forward to those months.

Alone.

No one around me. No one but one other man who lives in isolation even further into the hills.

Scarecrow is like me. He needs no one and chooses to leave society behind. It is because of him that I know so much about the land I thrive on. He's a one-legged bastard who hates everyone but the Lord, and maybe tolerates me. Refusing modern medicine to receive a prothesis for his missing appendage, he chose to stuff the bottom half of his pant leg with straw and call it good. Scarecrow showed me the secrets of Heaven shrouded in the sagebrush-covered hills.

This city I drive through, however, is a Godless city on a flat, dried land. Desert filth all around with no hope of salvation.

And then I see her... again. Poor little girl sitting in her own filth cross-legged in a field of weeds in front of a dilapidated trailer.

Spawn of white trash.

Forsaken.

Every month, I see her. Every month she appears to be alone. Today is no different except that this time I slow my truck so I can get a better look. She's dirty. Dirtier than normal. Her blonde hair isn't brushed and may have never been. Her clothes are too small, and she wears no shoes. Her wide eyes are blue as they look up at me as I lurk by. They scream desperate to me. They holler hunger and need. They shout for help over and over, so accustomed to never being heard. Her eyes. Her sad little eyes.

I drive on. I have to. I can't stay. Sorry, little girl. I can't listen to those eyes. Not today. Not ever.

I get my supplies and drive home. Home. Focus. Get the hell out of this pit of sin. But then I see the little girl again. She hasn't moved. I suppose she has nowhere to move to. So, I stop. God help me. I stop.

Rolling down my window, I say, "What are you doing outside?"

She twists her head to look at the trailer she calls home. She then stares at me and shrugs.

"How old are you?"

She puts up five fingers.

"Where is your mommy? Your daddy?"

She shrugs. Her eyes grow even bigger as if they are screaming louder. So loud.

"Are you alone?"

She nods.

"How long have you been alone?"

She shrugs.

Those eyes of her demand. They command me to get out of the truck and walk over to where she still sits. She smells of urine and neglect.

"What's your name?"

"Ember," she answers with a slight whistle of air escaping from her two missing front teeth.

"Can you show me inside your house?" I say as I extend my hand for her to take.

Without pause, because why would a five-year-old fear anything at all, she places her tiny palm into mine. We walk to the trailer, and I wonder why I am. What do I expect to see? The front door is wide open, but I could see that from my truck.

"Where is your mommy?" I ask again as we enter the dirty tin can.

"She's not here. She left a long time ago. She said her boyfriend was taking her on a trip. I wanted to go, but she said no. She said no kids allowed." Her voice is fragile and so delicate that the timbre nearly splinters my soul.

I glance around the front room. Empty beer cans and discarded needles scatter the stained floor. Flies swarm around crusty plates painted with dried food. I walk straight to the refrigerator and open the door. It's empty although I don't expect to see anything but. I open the cabinets and find them bare as well.

"When is the last time you ate?" I ask.

She shrugs again. Her eyes beg to be fed. Her eyes... her eyes...

"Are you hungry?"

"Yes, please." She's not old enough to be afraid of me, but old enough to have manners. Although by the looks of her upbringing, she was never *taught* how to behave. It just shows that children are born good and pure until corrupted by the evil ways of man.

"Are you all alone?" I already know the answer, but I suppose I need to hear the reply from her tiny, chapped lips.

"Mommy said someone would come and get me soon. She said to just sit outside every day and a person would come." She walks up to me and takes my hand again and squeezes tightly. So tight that I doubted I would ever be able to free my hand again. "She was right. You came."

Dear Lord, drown the bells in my heart. Silence the whispers in my mind.

"Yes, child. I've come."

4

CHRISTOPHER

HEAT FLOODS MY MUSCLES AS I STRUGGLE AGAINST the confines. A metal, cold shackle surrounds my ankle as if I'm cast back in the days of medieval times. I stifle the urge to scream but don't want to waste the sound without knowing my surroundings. My pulse speeds and alarms blare.

The room is dimly lit by an oil lamp in the furthest corner, too far for me to reach with the short length of chain hooked to the iron cuff holding me captive. I can see a door, a small window toward the ceiling that with my six-foot height I can maybe peer out of if I can get the chain to extend, which based on how long I have tried to free myself, seems unlikely. There is no sunlight shining through the dirty glass, which tells me I have been knocked out for hours and night has already fallen. There are crates against the wall opposite of me, but still too far for me to utilize in any way to aid in my escape. The dank, dusty air, the dirt-covered floor, and the cool temperature of the room leads me to believe I'm in a cellar or a basement. The painful pounding on the back of my head reveals the story of how I ended up chained to the floor in a foreign place.

But where is my attacker?

Why am I here?

The unknown answers are nearly as terrifying as my current situation.

I can stand and take two steps before the chain stops me. I sit down and tug on the chain some more, but it is anchored into concrete. My ankle is bloody from all the fruitless effort rubbing it raw.

I need to regain my senses. I need to stay level-headed and focused. It's clear that I won't be able to break free from my constraints on my own, so I need to find another solution.

Footsteps approach the other side of the aged and discolored wooden door. Standing again, I widen my stance to prepare. When the door opens, I ready myself for war. A man walks in who, after a few moments, I recognize as the ranger of Hallelujah Junction. He's the last man I spoke to before... before...

He still wears his uniform of tan khaki with a state forestry patch on the shirt, or I wouldn't have come to the realization so quickly. On his heels is a thin, tiny blonde woman, though I have to question if she's truly a woman or a girl. I do see breasts, however, barely visible beneath her oversized, dirty, floral dress that hangs on her like a child playing dress up with her mother's clothing. Her eyes are wide, her cheeks sunken slightly, and her long blonde hair hangs down her back weaved in a braid.

Neither of them seems surprised to see me awake. The shadows of the room conceal the finer details of both of their appearances, but I can now see who are responsible for me being shackled to the floor. The ranger stares at me directly, but the woman does not. She fixes her eyes at the ground before her, biting her lip and wringing her hands.

"Christopher Davenport," the man says as they fully enter the room.

I reach for my back pocket and notice my wallet is missing.

"115 57th Street, New York, New York. Staff photographer for *Rolling Stone Magazine*. Chiefly known for his portraits of the rich, the infamous, and the powerful but also freelances with additional photo credits in other magazines like *National Geographic*. Son of wealthy socialite Louisa Davenport and only heir to the Davenport textile empire," the ranger says as if reciting a book report. He clearly has researched me based on my I.D. he now possesses.

"What the fuck do you want?" I rasp. My hands are free from restraint. He will soon regret that decision.

Take a step closer, motherfucker.

Come on. Step closer.

Is this a ransom situation? When traveling overseas and in dangerous countries, the reality of something like this happening is a possibility and one I am always aware of. But not in the United States. Not in Nevada off the beaten path.

"You've traveled a long distance to be here," the ranger says as he stands in front of the crates directly before me. The woman is still near the doorway as if entering the room is too dangerous.

"I don't know why you did this, but if it's money you want—"

"Money is the root of all evil," the man interrupts. "That is the last thing that my daughter and I want."

I track my eyes to his *daughter* and question those words. She doesn't look anything like the man, nor does she seem particularly comfortable in his presence. The dim light of the room, the calmness of the man speaking, the fear visible in the stance of the woman, have the tiny hairs on my nape standing on end.

"Then what the fuck do you want?" My voice snaps through the still and stagnant air.

He bends toward me, his face closer—but not

close enough for me to reach out and strangle—
and cast in haunting shadows. "Well, the first thing
I want from you is for you to watch your language.
There's a lady present, and I expect you to show
some respect."

My fist twitches.

Everything inside of me threatening to boil to a
point of epic disaster if I don't control my
emotions. I must stay calm. I must use my mind,
because I have no doubt I am smarter than the
man in front of me. Outwit over force considering
there is a metal chain restricting me from escaping.

I glance at the woman again. She swallows,
licks her lips, and continues to stare at the floor,
her weakness causing my blood to boil even more.

"I am a man who believes in asking and thou
shall receive," the ranger says. "My daughter,
Ember, is of marrying age. Some would say a few
years past. It's my responsibility to arrange a
suitable and Godly partnership for her. Up to this
point, I have failed her in this regard. But I suppose
you could say that I'm picky. I don't believe in love
at first sight, dating, playing the field and all the
other foolish and sinful ways of today's belief. The
only love that needs to exist for union, is the
mutual love for God."

He holds his palm out to his daughter, waiting.

Something flickers in her blue eyes as she
stares at him.

Comprehension.

Fear.

Reality.

She eventually moves to take his hand and twists her body to face me head on. We share a look, and in that moment of time, I have hope. She doesn't want to be here. She doesn't want *me* to be here.

I can see it.

I can feel it.

"Although you are not prepared to be her husband yet. Far from worthy in the eyes of the Lord. But I do believe I can groom you during the courting of my daughter," he continues, though his words are not entering my mind as they should. I can't make sense of the madness spewing from his lips. "And though Ember has no momma to guide her, she is a good girl and can learn quickly."

"Papa Rich," Ember says tentatively, "I don't—"

"Silence!" His lip curls as he seethes his venom. He reaches out and strikes her upside the head, causing her to tighten her fists in front of her, focusing on the floor in complete silence. He straightens his shoulders as he takes a deep breath. "My apologies. My daughter is usually much more submissive and obedient. She normally does not talk out of turn. But I assure you I will school her in the ways of being a proper bride as I groom you in your duties as a husband. I give you my word as a man I will take my responsibilities seriously."

Ember's face reddens with a quick glance my way, and she stares back down toward her hands as her brows pull together.

"You want me to marry your daughter?" I ask. Even saying the words seem unreal. I feel as if I am floating in muddy water, suffocating, struggling to hold on to life.

Ember peers at me through her thick lashes. Her face is now a sheet of white, her chin quivering in anticipation of what can possibly come next. I wonder if she is a mirror, reflecting my internal struggle with my new reality.

"Not immediately," he says casually. "I do believe a proper time is required for courting."

"You hit me over the head, knocked me out"—I lean toward him as a raging fire erupts inside of me —"to marry your daughter?"

I have never killed a man. Never considered it before now. Now... I will.

"Correction," he says, crossing his arms under his chest. "I hit you over the head as a consequence for your rule breaking. You were trespassing. But then, God spoke to me. Rather than dragging your body to its death, I spared you. I am offering the hand of my daughter to you. You should be grateful."

I lurch forward, determined to inflict pain and

massive amounts of blood. "You sick motherfucker!" The chain prevents me from reaching him, throws me off balance, and forces me to my knees.

The ranger charges me in instant retaliation but freezes in his tracks. I brace myself for the punch to the face, in fact, I welcome it. Something, anything but this insanity I'm thrust into. I slam my fist down, hard enough to make Ember gasp and scurry toward the door.

"You want to kill me?" I shout. "Go for it, you sick fuck."

He straightens to his full height and takes a few steps back. Without removing his eyes from mine, he crooks a finger at Ember. She wipes away traces of tears from her eyes and walks back to where she once stood by his side.

"I'm going to leave you and Ember for a while so you both can become acquainted with each other better. I don't feel your initial meeting should be with me hovering over you both."

"You can't keep me down here," I begin. "People know where I am. It's just a matter of time until the authorities will be combing every inch of this fucked-up town looking for me."

A slow-growing smile forms on his face. "It's a shame that you fell to your death in the acid pits. It happens every year, sadly. People get careless as they take pictures and not pay attention to all the warning signs. It's a dangerous, dangerous place here in Hallelujah Junction. You should see the amount of paperwork it causes me, but the local police are aware it's just part of our environmental hazards. But then again, if you had only followed the rules, you would still be alive. I did recover pieces of your camera near the pits, however. So, your family may be able to have some sense of closure, though we will never know if you tripped, or if a beam or floorboard gave way. No real way of knowing considering the shoddy condition the old mill is in. And a body will never be found of course, not with the way the acid will fry your flesh and bone to nothing. But your poor, poor mother. I'm sure she was always worried your job was too dangerous. I'm sure she always wished you would have just taken over the family business. If only she had not bought you your first camera when you were a child." His smile never leaves his face. "Shame. Shame. Another young soul has lost his life. Shame."

"You plan on keeping me locked up down here forever?" I ask.

Cords twang in his neck as he looks over his shoulder at Ember. His smile never deflates. "Of course not. I have a plan, son. A plan for our future."

"Plan?"

"No worries to you both. I'll be a good father-in-law. I know kids these days need a leg up, and I'll provide this to the both of you." He puts up his palm to stop me from speaking. "And yes, I know you aren't quite a kid. You are older than my Ember, but I do believe she is an old soul, and though she is only twenty-five, she will be able to match you as a partner. And I'm old fashioned. I believe having an older man to help guide his wife is beneficial to any union."

"I don't care what you do to me, but I won't do this," I say as I sit back as if the air has been punched out of me. I wish I sounded stronger. I should be standing. I should be acting as if the man should fear *me*. But I can barely breathe.

"But you will," he states. He walks to the frightened woman and pats her on the head. "I'm going to leave you alone for now. You watch over him like a good girl, you hear?"

She hesitates, her eyes locked on me, but then she nods.

"Welcome, Christopher. My name is Richard, this here is Ember. We'll be your new family. Your only family."

He leaves. The door closes.

I lower my voice for only her ears. "You need to help me get out of here." I lift my leg to show her the metal cuff. "Do you know where he keeps the key?"

Her forehead pinches and her lips part. "Don't anger him."

"Okay, listen to me. I know you're scared. But we need to act fast while he's gone." Hysteria, anxious need, and downright fear have me pleading with the girl to listen.

She remains in place.

"Ember is it? You need to help me. To help yourself."

Deep breath. Deep breath. Reason with her. Don't scare her.

"I don't want to get into trouble," she says.

"You won't get into any trouble. You didn't do this, and I will tell the police that. But you need to help me escape."

"Papa Rich will get mad if he knew you were talking like this." She takes a few steps away from me, her eyes locked on the door.

I want to strangle her yet rescue her at the same time.

Deep breath. Deep breath. She's a wild animal. Afraid.

"We both can leave here together. I promise I won't let anything happen to you." I stroke her with my words. Hoping. Praying.

"Why would I want to leave?" she asks. "This is my home."

"He's crazy! This is pure insanity. He kidnapped me. Don't you see that?"

She tenses and changes her breathing. "He didn't kill you like I thought he would. So, that means he must like you. It shows he really means what he says and wants you to be part of our family."

Oh. My. Fucking. God.

She is as crazy as he is.

I stand again, hoping my height and dominant presence might intimidate her enough for her to at least fear me a little. "You need to get me out of here." The words are harsh, forceful, unforgiving. They are delivered like a rapid firing of a gun.

"Please stop asking me to," she says. "Even if I could..." Whatever drifts through her mind distracts her to silence.

But then... it appears that she considers.

Her footsteps approach. Not close enough for me to reach out to her, but close enough that I could see the tremble in her lip, the tears blurring the blue in her eyes, and the wisps of blonde curls framing her face. She's so much shorter than me, her head only reaching the height of my shoulder, and her bare feet don't give her any added height from the addition of shoes.

"Papa Rich is a fair man," she says. "As long as you don't fight him, and you follow his rules, everything will be all right. He won't harm you."

"He can't keep me here. He wants to force me to

marry you. He's crazy and dangerous. You have to see that."

"He's my father…"

"I understand how hard this must be," I say softly, hoping I can reason with her rather than forcing her to run away from me. "But he needs help. If you let me go, we can do whatever it takes to get him the kind of help he needs. We can all be happy."

"He just wants me to be married. Isn't it part of growing up?"

"Ember!" Her name is shouted from outside the room. It's muffled but loud. "Come join me upstairs. We have company!"

Her eyes dart to the door, and then back at me. "I have to go. But I promise when I return, I'll make you comfortable. I'll do good by you. I promise."

"Wait! Don't leave," I say as I desperately reach out to her but come nowhere close to actually touching skin on skin.

She runs to the door leaving me standing there in my own despair.

"I'll be back as soon as I can, Christopher. I know you don't like this, but I'll make it all better. Somehow I will." She leaves the room and softly closes the door behind her.

5

THE STENCH OF CHEAP WHISKEY, SPOILED ONION, and body odor roots me in place.

Scarecrow.

He's here.

He never announces his arrival, and we never know how long between visits, but it does seem as if he was here not that long ago. Why Papa Rich likes him, when he hates all other people, baffles me.

Papa Rich sees me in the doorway of the kitchen and motions me to enter. "I was just telling Scarecrow that we have a houseguest."

I don't want to look at Scarecrow, but his heavy breathing and thumping of his crutch against the planked floor forces me to. His agitated state confuses me.

"This isn't right, Richard, and you damn well know it. She was promised to me," Scarecrow says.

Papa Rich calmly leans against the wooden counter we prepare all our meals on. It's scarred with years of neglect and abuse, but clean and built well. The counter will forever hold his weight. "I never made the promise she would marry you."

"You did!" Scarecrow snaps.

"I said if I could not find a suitable husband for Ember, I would *then* allow you to marry her. But as I have just informed you, I have found a suitable man who will take her hand in marriage. You won't be needed to step in."

My pulse spikes, but at the same time, relief cascades down my spine. I didn't realize any such deal had been made between them. The thought of marrying Scarecrow makes me ill. He's greasy, stinky, and meaner than a trapped and provoked hornet.

"Who?" Scarecrow asks as spittle escapes from his chapped and canker sore-riddled lips. "You know that she's different. *We* are different. And she should marry me!" He slams his crutch against the floor again, and our teacups and china plates I have stacked on a shelf to the right of the sink rattle.

I worry they will fall to the ground and shatter, and then we will be without. Papa Rich won't replace the pretty things. I have one chance to keep the pretty close, or the practical will take over. But I won't approach Scarecrow to save them from falling either. I see he has something crusty and dark on his flannel shirt. I can't tell if it is dried blood or fecal matter.

The man is contamination in all ways.

"I will help you find a proper wife," Papa Rich says. "God will speak to the both of us and let us know who that woman will be."

"Who do you think you are speaking to?" Scarecrow leans forward, and the movement causes loose straw to fall out of his pant hem that is tied with a mud-stained piece of rope. His hay-stuffed leg sways back and forth with the movement. "*I* am the preacher in these parts. Don't you start speaking about the Lord to me. Not to *me*!"

"I understand you're disappointed."

"We had an agreement. A handshake."

Papa Rich nods but still remains calm regardless of the rage before him. "I have not gone against my word. I said from the beginning that if I didn't find a proper husband who—"

"Who is this man you consider better than me?" Scarecrow bellows. "Show him to me."

"In due time."

"Where is he?"

Papa Rich resettles his weight from one foot to the other but never breaks his steady positioning. "When I feel the time is near, I'll send word to you.

I do ask you, my friend, to preside over the wedding. It would mean the world to me to have your pronouncement forever bind them together."

Scarecrow crosses his arms against his chest and huffs. "You have some nerve."

Papa Rich chuckles. "Call it what you will, but I want the best for my daughter."

Scarecrow shoots angry eyes my way for the first time. "Is this what you want, girl?"

I say nothing. Does he expect me to declare I want Scarecrow as my husband instead of Christopher? Those words will never leave my mouth.

Scarecrow redirects his attention back to Papa Rich and points with a dirty, mangled finger missing a nail. "You better make good on your word and find me a bride, Richard. You better make good."

Banging from downstairs, followed by the shouts for help from Christopher pull all of our attentions to the stairway.

My heart skips, my fingertips flutter against my lips. I worry for the man below. He's not listening to Papa Rich. He's not following the rules.

I also worry for me. If Papa Rich gets angry and takes Christopher to the acid pits, then it means I will have to marry Scarecrow instead.

I would rather throw myself in the pits than even touch the vile man before me.

Scarecrow shakes with laughter. "Is this the groom you speak of? The man hollering for help?" He wipes at the spit escaping his mouth. "I think you've lost your damned mind, but I'll be a good friend regardless." He looks directly at me. "But if you change your mind and want a Godly man who can provide as a husband of yesteryear once did, then I'll always welcome my home and bed to you. I give my word on that."

He could have punched me in the gut, and the same effect would occur. I have to actually focus on not doubling over as the air seems to rush out of me.

Christopher continues to shout his demands from downstairs. I feel sorry for him. If he thinks that Scarecrow is the kind of man who would actually care or help a person chained up against his will in a cellar, then he is sorely mistaken.

Scarecrow shakes his head in disbelief and moves toward the door to leave but stops and looks over his shoulder at Papa Rich. "How long do you plan on keeping the man locked up down there?"

"That decision is up to him," Papa Rich answers simply. "In time, the man will be just as eager to marry Ember as I am to have her married."

"And if you're wrong?" Scarecrow challenges.

"This isn't about me. God spoke, and God is never wrong."

Limping past the threshold and finally leaving

our house, Scarecrow says, "I hope you listened correctly, and it was actually God speaking and not the Devil. Evil is alive and well, and it's ravenous as hell."

Help! Is anyone up there? Help, I'm down here! Help!

"Ember, go downstairs and quiet the man up," Papa Rich orders, but he still remains calm. I'm grateful that I don't see him angry... yet.

"Papa Rich?" I begin, risking not following his command right away. "Were you really going to have me marry Scarecrow?" I nearly whisper the words in fear that Scarecrow is still in earshot.

I truly had no warning, or even an inclination that it was a possibility, and I feel a sense of betrayal because of it.

He approaches me and strokes my cheek. "My sweet Ember. I would never make a decision that is not right for you. Nor would God. It's why that man downstairs was brought to us. I prayed the right person would someday come, and he did."

"I didn't know you wanted me to get married... now."

He continues to stroke my face like I stroke the head of my cat, Pine Cone. "It's time. No father wants to see his little girl grow up, but the day will always come."

"You want me to leave you?" I ask, sadness

filling my heart. We never discussed this. I had always assumed... my place is with Papa Rich.

"Never, my girl. Never. Hallelujah Junction is your home and will forever be your home. But you are such a beautiful girl and have so much to offer that we can't waste that gift."

"But you just *took* him."

"Yes, that is true. But God spoke to me. And even though the man downstairs doesn't know it yet, he is destined to be your husband. To join our family."

"Are we to live here in the main house? Married? Downstairs? My room? What if he says no? He can't stay chained up forever."

"Shh..." He still caresses my face. "These are my worries to carry. Not yours."

"But I don't understand."

"You will," he says, finally ceasing in his constant petting. "For now, I need you to focus on learning how to be a wife. You need to woo Christopher just as he woos you. Yes, many unions happen by arrangement only, and that is still a possibility if the Lord chooses that path for us. But I do want love for you. I would like to see that occur between the two of you if at all possible."

"Love?" Thoughts of all the romance novels I read and fantasize about in the schoolhouse rush in. I never thought love was a possibility as I turned those pages lost in the fairytale of true happiness. I am in hiding. I can't leave. I can't find love.

But did love find me?

"It will take time," he says as he leans against the counter as he had been while speaking with Scarecrow. "He may be resistant at first, and you may not know how to love anyone other than me. But I feel like it can happen if you both work hard enough."

His talk of love wraps around me like a warm hug. I want it. I want it so badly. More than anything in my entire life.

A husband.

A man to love me like the men in all the books love their women.

I want the happily ever after too.

Papa Rich is finally giving me a gift. A gift of love.

"Thank you, Papa Rich. I'll work really hard on being good and making Christopher want me as his wife."

Papa Rich nods his approval. "I know you will, child. I know you will."

The hollers come again from downstairs, followed by more pounding on the wall or ground, and even the rattling of the chain.

"But I won't ask you again," he says, his tone changing from light to dark. "Go silence him before he works my last nerve."

6

CHRISTOPHER

THE TINY WOMAN ENTERS THE ROOM AGAIN, AND ANY hope someone will hear my shouts for help is deflated. Someone was upstairs, and clearly did not hear me. Or maybe they did, and they were killed or tied up somewhere in their own prison.

"You have to be quiet," Ember says as she places her thin finger to her lips.

"Who was up there?" I'm sitting but consider standing to bulldoze her fragile state of mind with my stance but choose to wait and see how she reacts. I don't want to chase her away, because I truly feel she may be my only chance at escape, as thin as it is.

"Trust me," she says as she closes the door behind herself. "The man upstairs will not help you in any way. You don't want him down here." Her lips pinch, and her nose wrinkles.

I watch her walk completely across the room and light another lantern on a small table in a far corner. It reveals another door I hadn't seen before.

"There's indoor plumbing in the main house unlike the rest of the buildings in Hallelujah Junction," she says, pointing to the door. "There's a bathroom here, although the water heater doesn't work very well, so most likely the water will be cold." She glances at the chain around my ankle, restricting me from even going near the door. "I'm sure I can convince Papa Rich to give you a longer chain or something so you can use it."

Her voice is so soft. So delicate. Almost melodic.

"How long have you been here?" I ask as she sits on one of the crates before me—still out of reach.

Her eyes widen, and she tilts her head. "What do you mean?"

"He's not your father, is he?"

"He is."

I shake my head. "I don't believe he is."

She swallows hard and looks down at her fingertips. "He saved me. He's my father in the eyes of God, and that's all that matters."

The way she recites the sentence tells me that she's been fed the line of crap for so long she actually believes it. I can't help but feel she is a lost lamb about to be devoured by wolves. Hell, she's already their evening meal.

"How long has he been your... father?"

"My mother left me when I was five. Papa Rich took me and raised me as his own." Her eyes lift and she stares at me head on. "I've never discussed this with anyone before. Actually... I've never discussed anything with anyone. You're the first person—besides my father's friend, whom I hate—that I have ever spoken to."

"Why?" I ask, feeling like I must get this woman to open up to me if I have any shot at convincing her to find the key to my shackles.

"I have to stay hidden," she says so softly, I have to lean forward to read her lips to help make sense of her words.

"Hidden?"

She looks at the door, pauses for a moment, and then refocuses her attention on me. "My mother is dangerous. If she knew I was here, she would come get me. My life would be at risk with her. Even now as an adult, she would still want me for revenge purposes alone. I'll never be safe. Papa Rich says she has people looking for me, and we can't trust anyone. No strangers. No one. So, my only chance of staying alive from the power and evil she has, is to stay hidden. He keeps me safe in Hallelujah Junction far away from most. He doesn't think she would ever look for me here, but we have to make sure by not allowing me to ever be seen by anyone."

Ember can't possibly believe the words she says, but it appears she does. She truly does.

"So, you came here to live when you were a child? How old are you now?"

"Twenty-five. But we don't celebrate birthdays. I read about them in books, but Papa Rich says that materialistic things are the root to evil, and birthdays are about presents, and we don't partake in the ways of modern man. We're different."

This poor woman. She was kidnapped twenty years ago and has been brainwashed by the crazy man upstairs. She's a victim just like me.

She just doesn't know it.

"So, you live in this house? Were you ever chained up like me?" I ask, trying to make sense of her situation. Speaking to her is like putting a puzzle together one piece at a time.

She smiles warmly and nods. "My father is the ranger in Hallelujah Junction. They give him this house which is up the road behind the schoolhouse. The visitors can't come up here where we actually live." She pauses and looks at my ankle shackled in metal. "Well... visitors aren't supposed to." She takes a deep breath and then looks back into my eyes. "There are underground tunnels that connect many of the buildings. They were built years and years ago by the miners who founded this town. Papa Rich trusts me to walk them so I can visit more buildings than just our home. The schoolhouse is my favorite because I like to read, and that's where we keep boxes of old books. My father teases me and tells me that someday, I'll read them all, but I still have a long way to go. I haven't opened all the boxes yet."

"Are you never allowed outside?" I rub my ankle, knowing that forcing my way out from these restraints is futile. But this woman... this woman can be my ticket to freedom.

"Not during tourist season." She glances at the door again. She's scared my captor will hear her. I can see it. Mental note: this *daughter* does fear her *father*. I can use that fact to my advantage. "But during the wintertime, the road up to Hallelujah Junction is usually closed due to the snow. So then, the entire town is ours. Papa Rich allows me to go outside then. I love it. We build snowmen, and even snowshoe for exercise. Winter is my favorite season because of the..."

Freedom, I want to answer for her but remain silent.

"I only visit the buildings that the tourists can't in the busy season," she adds.

An eerie realization dawns on me. "You're the female ghost in the schoolhouse window that makes Hallelujah Junction so famous, aren't you?"

She plays with the ends of her hair and nods.

"It was an accident. I didn't know I could be seen. When Papa Rich found out that people saw me, he was so angry. He told me I had to stay here in the cellar like you. It was a long time before he let me out."

I exhale a lungful of air I didn't realize I was holding.

She twists her hair around and around her index finger. "But he eventually let me out of this room. He taught me when it was okay to be in the school window and when it wasn't. He said my accident actually protects me even more. Because if I am somehow seen again, he can blame the ghost and folklore getting in the minds of people hoping to see the schoolhouse haunting."

I reposition my body, and as I do, I see this woman in a completely different way.

The darkness of the room that drips and oozes with diabolical acts drowns by the warmth in her voice. "I'm the ghost of Hallelujah Junction," she adds, and I can't tell if that last statement makes her proud or sad.

I carefully consider how I proceed with Ember. My earlier attempt of trying to reason with her didn't work. Whether I understand it or not, she loves her kidnapper. I can't expect her to give up years and years of believing the man is her savior by simply telling her she's wrong. He has earned her trust, devotion, and loyalty. My only chance is somehow overpowering those feelings and emotions with her own toward me. How? I am not sure. But somehow.

"Are you hungry? Thirsty?" she asks.

"Not yet." I can't accept the fact that I will be down here long enough to even consider food and water.

"I'm a good cook. Or at least Papa Rich says so. I found several old cookbooks in the schoolhouse that I use, although I have the recipes memorized now. Is there anything special you like to eat?"

Her smile is slow building, but when it fully forms, her appearance completely changes. She doesn't appear nearly as haunted as before.

Jesus. She's so hopeful she can actually please me in my current situation.

"Ember..." I proceed with caution. "Have you ever wanted to leave Hallelujah Junction?"

"My mother—"

"If you could be protected from her," I cut in, validating her concern. "If *I* could protect you from her."

"As my husband?" she asks almost whimsically. Like I was her found Prince Charming and could slay all the dragons.

I can't say yes, but I also don't want to lose her. "I would protect you."

Ember hops off the crate she is sitting on and takes a few cautious steps toward me. I wouldn't reach out and grab her even if I could. I can already tell this process of convincing her to release me will take small baby steps.

"What can we do to make you more comfortable?" she asks. "I can get blankets and pillows if that helps."

I bite back the bubbling fury building inside of me. I want to snap, to yell, to shake sense into her that no amount of pillows or blankets are going to make me comfortable, but she will run. I know she will run.

"A chair," I say, shaking off my frustration. "So, I don't have to sit on the ground."

Her eyes light up, and that smile of hers returns. She quickly runs around a crate and drags a wooden chair from behind it. She doesn't pause before reaching me this time, which I take as a good sign. If I wanted to, I could grab her and snap her neck with my bare hands. But she is unaware of that fact which tells me the trust level is beginning.

She places the chair beside me, and I stand. She still doesn't move or take any steps backwards. She doesn't even flinch.

"Thank you," I say softly.

We are close enough now that I can see more defined features of her appearance. Though I had originally thought her dirty based mostly on her attire and our surroundings, I could now see she is very clean. Oddly so, considering she was barefoot in a dirty cellar. Her nails are short, but no dirt caked underneath them. Her blonde hair shines bright as if freshly washed. Even her dress isn't dirty... worn... but not dirty.

Her eyes are bluer than any eyes I have ever seen. They stand out the most on her nearly angelic face. She's smaller than most women, and skinnier but not necessarily malnourished or starving. *Stunted*, would be a word best to describe her. Almost as if her body is brainwashed—just like her mind—to believe she is an innocent child even though she is a grown woman.

"Ember." Saying her name feels odd. "Did your father tell you what his plans are?"

"In regard to our wedding?"

I nod as I take the seat and twist my body so I am looking right at her. "Or about me in general."

She takes a deep breath and closes her eyes for a brief moment. "He hasn't told me much. I didn't know he wanted me to be married. I didn't know this was the plan. He's told me to allow him to worry about all the details and to just focus on... us."

"Us?"

"On falling in love," she says with over-bright eyes filled with foolish beliefs.

I think up to this point, I never actually felt true panic. Not until this very moment.

Panic.

Fucking Hell...

Love? Love? *Love?*

The word seems absurd. The emotion seems deranged. Love and madness is my new reality, and all I can do is drown in my wave after wave of hysteria.

"I should really go and start supper," she says as she steps away from me for the first time since bringing me the chair.

I wonder if she can see the lunacy in my eyes. Can she see how it has finally hit me like a brick that I am held captive and may never escape? In a matter of hours, I will be dead to all who know me. They will have no reason to doubt the ranger that I fell to my death. They know I would always go the extra distance to get the perfect picture, even if it meant falling to my death in a pit of acid.

"I was going to make stew... if that is alright with you?" She wants my approval. She is nearly begging for it with those eyes of hers.

I have nothing left in me to continue on. Not now, and maybe not ever.

Jesus fucking Christ.

"Stew is fine," I mumble.

Fuck. Fuck. Fuck!

7

I HATE THE FACT I ACTUALLY ALLOWED MYSELF TO sleep last night. I even hate myself more for eating the stew Ember made and settling into the pillows and blankets she brought me as a dutiful hostess would do.

I should fight more. I should not allow any acceptance of this situation.

The bright light shining through the window only reminds me it is now official. In the real world, I am a missing man.

My editor will be waiting for me to send photo proofs. I'm pretty sure I have a lot of unread emails, unreturned text messages, and missed phone calls. My mother won't be particularly worried yet, since she has become accustomed to me not speaking to her every day. Although my sort of girlfriend,

Marissa, will no doubt think I am banging some other chick and currently be in the middle of a stream of texts ranting about what an asshole I am and how my failure to commit to her only proves I am a spoiled, silver spoon-fed momma's boy with no hope of ever finding true happiness. It's likely some will assume I'm on a bender, though not my work. No matter what, the workaholic in me has forced me to show up every day, meet every deadline, and act in the utmost professional manner. Odd, that it will be my employer who will notice my disappearance and find it concerning before my mother or my... well... the woman I sleep with, will.

If any one of them knew I'm actually chained up, in a cellar, held captive by a psychopath grooming me to marry his physically and mentally stunted kidnapped pretend daughter, they wouldn't believe it. Who could believe this? I'm struggling to grasp the reality myself.

I wonder if Richard is reading all of my texts and getting pleasure in watching my life implode one angry message at a time.

My poor mother, and not for the reasons one would think. This will be all the gossip and really hurt her socialite status. The pity in the eyes of all her lunch date besties will truly eat her alive. The hushed rumors, the well wishes laced with hidden agendas just to dig for more gossip. Her invites to parties will decrease because no one wants a dark cloud to attend a gala. And of course, she won't be able to hold a proper funeral for me where she can wear a ten-thousand-dollar designer black dress and dab her eyes with a handkerchief once belonging to some queen of another country and considered a priceless antique. She will not be able to have all eyes on her as she throws her body over my open casket declaring she doesn't know how she can go on without her only son.

She will feel cheated that there is no body for her handsome son. I'm sure I would make for a very attractive corpse in an expensive, custom-fitted suit.

Oh yes... my poor mother.

I rub the sleep from my eyes and find it odd I'm still a little groggy.

The stew...

There must have been something in the stew Ember cooked to knock me out. No way could I have slept through the night on a cold cellar floor without some sort of sedative. Especially since I can't remember the last time I went to bed without several glasses of whiskey and two or three sleeping pills. My nighttime cocktail is my way of life, and I don't judge myself nor do I give a shit who does.

I do me. Do I drink more than mother dearest would approve of and pop pills like a child in a candy store with free samples? Damn straight. And when this entire nightmare is over, I will throw myself a true rager to attempt to erase the awful memories of this medieval dungeon from my mind. It may take me never being sober again to forget this ordeal.

But for now, all I can do is get off the ground to sit on my chair of dignity. It's how I see this chair. At least I am not on the floor like some animal.

My throne.

For I am now the king overseeing the demented, the unhinged, and the stark raving madness of this depraved empire.

I notice the chain to my ankle cuff is longer. A lot longer.

This must have happened while I slept in a drug-induced stupor.

Standing up and testing the length, I can see this Richard fuck is smarter than I give him credit for. I can make it to the bathroom, which I use instantly, and I can make it around the room for the most part. But I can't reach the doorway to escape at all. Richard will be able to stand by the door, and I can't reach him to strangle him to death. I can also reach the wall with the window, but barely. There isn't enough slack for me to stand on a crate or chair to look out of it. It's like this asshole measured every single inch of this room and read my mind on what I would do once I knew he gave me enough slack to move more freely.

"How did you sleep?" I hear a soft voice from behind me ask as I stare up at the window. I didn't notice Ember enter the room.

"I think you know the answer to that since you drugged me," I say as I walk back to my chair.

"Papa Rich said it would make you more comfortable." She takes a few cautious steps toward me and points to the chain. "He said if I sprinkled the stew with the powder, he would give you more length so you can use the restroom."

I don't say anything but take in her appearance instead. She's wearing another floral dress that seems to fit her better. The fabric is still worn, and the hem that reaches below her knee is frayed. She is still barefoot, her hair remains in a braid down her back, but her face seems to have more color. More life. The rosy color in her cheeks only brightens the blue in her eyes more. She is actually a very pretty woman, especially considering she clearly gets no assistance from salons or plastic surgeons like all the women I'm used to seeing in New York.

Her wide eyes are full of worry, and her fingertips touch her collarbone. "Are you mad at me?"

Such a simple question.

Such a normal question.

"There are a lot of people worried about me right now," I say, examining her closely to see how she reacts to my statement.

She looks to her feet. I see guilt. Good.

"Do you have a big family?" She lifts her eyes and looks at me through long eyelashes. "Brothers and sisters?"

"No brothers or sisters, but I have a mother who I'm close with. I have friends and coworkers who no doubt are scared." I consider telling her of Marissa too, but I do worry that if Richard finds out, he may just kill me and find another poor fool to go through this absurd *courting*. I need to stay alive long enough to somehow figure out a way to escape.

"Being an only child is lonely," she says as she walks to the same crate she sat on yesterday. Sitting, she crosses her legs, leans forward, and locks her stare on me.

"I suppose so."

"What is *Rolling Stone*? Papa Rich says that's where you work."

I swallow hard to force down the growing frustration. She's acting like we are on a date learning about each other when what a normal woman would be doing is helping me come up with a plan to run away.

"It's a magazine. I take pictures for it." I have no idea if she even knows what a magazine is.

"I saw your camera when you first arrived." She weaves her fingers together and looks down at them. "It broke when Papa Rich—"

"Can you stop calling him that?" I snap. "You aren't a child. It makes you come across as..." I take a deep calming breath. "You do realize you are a grown woman, right?"

Her eyes narrow, and I see her breathing change. She stiffens her spine, and the rosy hue in her cheeks pale. She stands. "I'll go cook you something for breakfast. Pap—my father has already left for work down the hill, so it's just us today."

She goes to the door, and I try to stop her. "Wait. I'm sorry. I didn't mean to sound so mean. It's just that—"

She opens the door and leaves without saying another word.

I look around the room and consider all options again and again. I could try to break a crate and use the splintered wood as a weapon. But against who? As frustrating as Ember is, I'm not going to harm the woman. I really feel deep down that she is just as much a captive as me. I haven't seen Richard since the first meeting, and I can already tell the man is smart. I highly doubt he will come close enough for me to use any form of violence in my favor. Not only isn't the chain long enough to allow me to climb on a crate to see through the window, I'd never fit through the rectangular opening if I were to break the glass. I already screamed for help, and that got me nowhere.

Fuck. Fuck. Fuck.

There is a high possibility a search party would be called to look for me. Unless somehow the crazy man is actually able to convince authorities I fell to my death like he claims he can. But without being able to see out the window, I won't know when to shout and make as much ruckus as I can. I'm not foolish enough to be at it all hours of the day. Pushing the patience of an unstable man isn't wise, and I would rather not be killed for testing the limits too far.

Ember.

She's my only chance of getting out of here—I know this, and I keep telling myself this and yet, I'm failing at actually listening. And I just successfully pissed her off. She wants to trust me. She wants to like me. I can see she wants to prove herself to her fucked up Papa Rich and be the perfect wife in this sick world they live in. She desperately wants me to be the Prince Charming she reads about in her books in that haunted shack of a schoolhouse.

Fucking with a woman's mind is not how I roll.

It never has been. I have always said it like it is, to the point where I can be considered an asshole. But I have always preferred to be a straight forward asshole rather than a slimy, lying prick. I don't do pick-up lines. I don't tell a woman what she wants to hear just to get in her pants. I don't bang chicks for the mere sport of it.

But here I am.

I have no choice but to fuck with this poor woman's mind if I ever want to escape. I have to play this demented chess game. Except in this game, I'm nothing but a weak pawn.

Fuck. Fuck. Fuck.

My hands shake and my head pounds. I need coffee. Actually, I need a shot of whiskey, a few uppers to help me face my day, but I'll settle for coffee to try to take this edge off.

I look at the door and figure that Ember will be returning soon with breakfast. I need to do a better job and can't scare her away anymore. I need her on my side.

Getting up and walking to the bathroom to clean up, I mentally prepare for what will no doubt be the hardest thing I will ever do in my life. I know I am highly intelligent—an attribute that has always benefitted me in my life. I'm also a fighter— another quality that has served me well. Yes, I'm chained in a cellar in an old mining ghost town, soon to be presumed dead. But I'm not going to throw in the towel. Not yet.

Richard will regret the day he chose me to marry his daughter. I'll make damn fucking sure of it.

8

CONCENTRATING ON NOT DROPPING THE TRAY OF food, I somehow open the door and enter with Pine Cone close at my heels. She's not used to ever being without me, nor all my attention not being focused on her. I keep my eyes on the scrambled eggs, bacon, and toast, not really wanting to look directly at Christopher. He makes me uncomfortable, and I don't know if I am scared of him, like him, hate him, or feel bad for him. All I know is my knees want to buckle as I enter the room.

"I wasn't sure how you liked your eggs," I say as I reach back with my foot and close the door shut.

"Please tell me what's inside that mug is coffee," he says which makes me look up and see he has a smile on his face. He also has washed off the dirt on his exposed skin and has rinsed the matted blood from his hair.

"It's black, but I can get cream or sugar if you want."

I hope he doesn't want sugar because I have very little of it, and I want to save what I do possess so I can make a cake later as a special treat. Papa Rich doesn't make a supply run for a few days, and I doubt he will make any exceptions.

"Black is perfect. So is scrambled. I'm not picky."

I let out the breath I'm holding, and hand him the tray. Not sure if I should remain in the room or not, I look for my cat. She has jumped up on the crate I sat on last time I was in the room. It's like she is making the decision for me. So, I sit.

"I didn't put anything in the food," I inform, although I quickly regret saying it as I see his body tense. But I also don't want him doubting every bite as he eats.

"What's your cat's name?" he asks as he drinks from the coffee first.

"Pine Cone," I answer as I pet the top of her gray head, needing the sound of her content purr to ease my discomfort. I'm not used to sharing air space with another, especially during the day while Papa Rich is at work.

"I'm sorry," he says with a mouthful of eggs. "I

didn't mean to snap at you like I did. I'm sure you can understand my frustrations."

"I do. I was down here for a long time once. And... I sometimes have to come to the cellar and be very, very quiet during inspection times. My father wants to make sure that I'm not spotted by anyone during the yearly State inspections."

"How long until they do another inspection?"

I know why he is asking, but I don't blame him. "They were just here about a month ago. So, another year is when we can expect a visit. They don't deviate from the schedule... or at least not since I've lived here."

"While you were upstairs cooking, I was thinking."

I don't say anything but run my fingers through Pine Cone's fur to soothe me. This man makes me nervous, and I need any help I can not to start shaking exactly where I sit.

"So, if we get married"—he takes a drink of coffee—"*when* we get married, I will need to still work and provide for our family." He looks at me seriously, the steam from the coffee circling around his face as he sips. "I can't do my job from here. My office is in New York, and I travel a lot to get the pictures I need. You understand that once we are wed, I can't stay here. *We* can't stay here. Right?"

My heart skips and the overwhelming... euphoria... nearly closes my airway. He wants to provide. He said the word *family*. He is talking marriage and our future.

"I'm sure Papa Rich has—"

"Let me tell you something about men. It's in our nature to provide." He bites into the bacon and pauses as I see his eyes search my face. "A strong man wants to lead his family. I understand that your father is the head of the household for you currently. But, when we get married, that role changes. *I* will be your husband. *I* will have to make decisions that are best for us. You understand that, I'm sure."

Did I? I suppose it makes sense that Christopher would want to be the one in charge. Not my father.

"We don't have to make a final decision right now," he says, which puts my swirling mind at ease a little. "I just want to plant the seed. That we do have to discuss our future and my career eventually. I can't provide for you financially and keep a roof over our heads unless I work. And I can't do that here."

"I don't think Papa Rich will allow us to leave," I say, scared that I will upset Christopher again because I like this new side of him I'm seeing.

But rather than his eyes darkening, and his jaw tightening like I am getting used to seeing, he smiles again. "We can plan all that later. It's always hard for parents to let go of their children and allow them to go and spread their wings. I get that. We don't have to tell him our plans yet. Let's just wait on that. Let him get used to the fact that another man is about to *steal his daughter away...* so to speak. Even though he wants you to get married, this is still going to be really tough for him. So, we can keep all our marriage talk between us for now."

"But what about Hallelujah Junction, and my mother?"

"I promise you that your mother will not be an issue. No matter where we go, she won't be. I give you my word. I come from a family with a lot of money and a lot of resources. On top of all that, I make my own income and can hire the best security and guarantee that you never have to hide again. As for this town, well..." He takes the last bite of food and chews it slowly before continuing. "Just like the miners who built this town. They all had to leave their homes and their families to start anew. It's part of life and has been happening since the beginning of time. I'm sure you've read about it countless times in all those books of yours."

True. I have. He has a very good point.

"I've never been to New York." I glance down at Pine Cone who is asleep by my side. I briefly remember simpler times when it was just my pet and me together in our isolation as we waited for the hours of the day to tick by. My face heats with shame as I add, "I've never been anywhere."

"You'll love it. It may take some getting comfortable to the idea since it's so different than what you're used to, but we could build a great future together. I'll buy you a home, and you can decorate it however you want to." He points to Pine Cone as he leans over and places the tray on the floor, keeping the coffee cup in his hand. "You can bring your cat, of course."

"She's my best friend," I admit.

"Which is sad," Christopher says, harsher than how he's been speaking. He quickly smiles to conceal the momentary... judgment of my situation, but I saw it. I saw the flash in his eyes before he could hide it from me.

The euphoria I was feeling only seconds ago is suddenly suffocated by something much darker.

Skepticism.

Doubt.

Suspicion.

I tilt my head and examine how easily Christopher crosses his legs and leans back in the wobbly wooden chair. He cups the mug of coffee and appears so... calm. Night and day difference from the man this morning.

This isn't real.

He isn't real.

An act. And I should know all about acts. I have gotten very good at them.

"Why are you lying to me?" I ask, hating that the words have to come from my lips. I want to believe. So badly, I want what he says to be true. "I'm not stupid, Christopher. I know you must think I'm dumb, which I can understand. I can believe you hate me. I can believe you can't stand that I'm sitting in this cellar and doing nothing to help you. But what I can't believe is what you are telling me now." I lean forward and bite the quiver out of my lip. "You don't have to lie to me."

For the first time since arriving with breakfast, I see an honest emotion in his eyes that he doesn't bother to enshroud in false promises and impossible dreams.

Hatred.

I clearly see hatred.

"Ember, what the fuck do you want me to say?" He swallows the last of his coffee and glares directly into my eyes. "Do I have a god damn choice? Huh? Daddy Dearest has declared we're getting married. So, it's a done deal."

"But you don't have to lie to me. You don't have to tell me I will someday have a home I can decorate, or how we'll someday have a family. If you don't mean it, you don't have to say it."

"Bullshit!" He throws the coffee cup across the room, and it shatters to pieces.

I jump and cower backwards but resist the urge to flee. He has the right to be angry. At least now, he's being honest. This is what I want. I don't want deceit. I want the real Christopher, no matter how awful the man could end up being. No matter how painful his words may be, I want them to at least be true.

He stands up and storms over to where I sit. The chain is long enough now. He can hurt me if he desires, but he stops inches from me with fisted hands.

"Do you want me to tell you I want to kill you? Because I don't. Do you want me to tell you I want to hurt you? That would be a lie too. I've already told you the truth. You know I want out of here. You know I want your help... that I *need* your help. I've already told you the fucking truth. Where has that gotten me?" He leans even closer, but his hands remain at his sides. I can feel his warm breath on my face. I feel his inner demons rage out of control, but his composed demeanor keep them at bay. "Huh? Tell me!"

He's shouting now, and though I want to run out of the room, scurry through the underground tunnels and retreat to my schoolhouse sanctuary, I feel I owe it to him to remain in place. I can't ask for the truth and then flee from it.

"What's going on here?" A voice I recognize well, slices through the tense air. Pine Cone snaps awake and darts behind the crates. She fears Papa Rich and has never warmed up to his presence.

Christopher remains where he's at but turns his head to face Papa Rich who stands in the doorway.

"We're just talking," I answer softly. I don't know why he's home from work. He rarely leaves the lower level of the town during open hours.

"It sounds like fighting," Papa Rich says, but he does not enter the room. His eyes are glued on Christopher as a stare down begins.

I'm surprised when Christopher breaks the tense connection and walks back to the chair and sits. "We were just discussing the future. You wanted me to get acquainted with my future bride, correct?" Venom drips from his words, but his body is casual and relaxed as he leans back and crosses his ankles as if he is at complete ease.

"I know the situation down here in the cellar is not ideal," Papa Rich says. "I understand why you look at me with such hate in your eyes. I don't blame you at all. But soon, you'll see why I've done what I've done."

"Is that what you think?" Christopher asks as he leans forward.

"It's what I know."

"You're wrong, madman. Wrong. You're going to have to kill me in here, you know that, right? Either that, or I'll escape. Somehow I will. Death or escape are my only two options and there is nothing you can do to change that. You may think you have all the control, but you're wrong." Christopher glances at me and adds, "You can't make me marry your daughter. You can't force this plan on me. I'll refuse. I'll choose death over letting you get your way."

"Tough guy I see," Papa Rich says calmly, but I'm barely breathing as I wait for his explosion of rage.

Christopher shrugs which I know is meant to infuriate Papa even more. "I speak the truth. You might hate hearing it, but it's reality. Are you prepared to kill me? Because that is what you'll have to do."

Papa Rich motions for me to stand by him, which I quickly do. I can feel something bad is brewing. I don't know what, or how, or when, but the hairs on my arms stand on edge in warning.

"Have you ever heard of the phrase *whipping boy*?" Papa Rich asks Christopher as I stand right by his side.

"I suppose I have."

"Good. But just to be certain you do, let me clarify. The whipping boy was used in the past to great effect. Corporal punishment was used on the unfortunate soul to keep a prince or a member of royalty in line who could not be disciplined themselves due to their status. To beat a dog before a lion. Watching another be beat for your transgressions would hopefully prevent you from doing the action again."

Papa Rich reaches for the buckle of his belt and begins to unfasten it. I've seen him do this before, but I have always done whatever it takes to avoid this action. For the most part, I succeed, and I worry about why he is removing his belt while his eyes are pinned on Christopher who hasn't moved an inch.

"Ember," Papa Rich begins, "lift your dress, bend over and touch your toes." He frees the belt completely, folds the belt in half, and snaps the leather.

My heart stops as confusion swamps my senses. "But, Papa—"

"Now, Ember."

I know better than to make Papa Rich repeat himself. The punishment will only be worse if I resist or beg for him not to. I also assume since there is an audience, he will have to prove a point if I am to embarrass him with my disobedience.

I am to show respect at all times. I know this.

Closing my eyes so I don't have to see Christopher as I bare myself, I do as directed. I hope the belting will be swift and not because of the pain but because of the embarrassment and shame of having to do such an act in front of Christopher.

"You are a strong man, Christopher." Papa

Rich's voice is calm but stern. "I can see that in you. So strong that if it became a battle of pure brute strength between us, it's likely you would win. So, there is only one solution to solve any *issues* between us. Ember will now be the whipping boy for you. If you break the rules, if you test my patience, or if you do anything I feel is worthy of correction, Ember will suffer the consequences as you watch. She will take the whipping *you* deserve for you." Papa Rich repositions my body by turning me around so my bare bottom is facing Christopher. "How severe, and how often your whipping boy is utilized is up to you."

I remain in position feeling the cool air of the room on my exposed flesh. I am not wearing panties and regret that decision. But the two pairs I do own are so tattered and thin they wouldn't have provided much coverage anyway.

I desperately want the lashing to begin. Stinging pain would be far better than the intense degradation I am feeling now. I may never be able to face Christopher again after this punishment. What must he think?

"You are a sick, sick man," I hear Christopher say.

"I am a man of conviction."

"You're insane for even thinking of this. And a coward. Who's to say I even care what you do to her?"

"You care," Papa Rich says. "No man would want to see an innocent girl pay for their crimes. I have a feeling it will just take a couple of lessons to truly keep you in line. Just know each whipping will be worse." The leather touches my skin, and then I can sense the belt is being raised behind me to prepare for the first strike. "But just to prove my theory that you'll make sure your whipping boy doesn't suffer my wrath often, let us begin."

9

CHRISTOPHER

Jesus fucking Christ. What do I do?

Do I try to stop him? But even if I charge him, I already know the chain doesn't reach where they stand. I'm also wise enough to realize storming toward them may help ease my conscience that I at least tried to stop this cruel act, but it will also only anger him more, and my *whipping boy* will pay for it rather than me.

"You want to whip someone, be man enough to try to whip me." I attempt not to look at the bare skin of the woman bent over for my viewing. She's owed her dignity, and I won't gawk at the display, yet at the same time, I feel I owe her the respect of not ignoring the situation by simply looking away.

I want to close my eyes, cover my ears, and scream from the top of my lungs, but I know it will only intensify the situation. I can't give this psychopath what he wants. He wants to break me. He wants me weak. He wants to see my fear.

The first strike lands firmly on her upturned ass. She squeals but holds her position even though her thighs quiver.

"I rarely have to punish Ember," Richards says as he raises his arm to prepare for the next assault. "You'll be a lucky man in that regard. You won't have to discipline her often, if at all."

This man...

He speaks as if it is completely normal to spank a grown woman.

This woman...

Remains in place and doesn't put up a fight as if she too believes this is the way of society.

Although a quick glance around at my nightmarish surroundings makes it quite obvious I'm trapped in a morphed reality. This is their world. Their twisted and distorted ordinary.

He whips her again, this time a cry escaping from her trembling frame.

I can't watch as he does it again and again, but I have to. I fear what will happen if I look away.

The whipping boy.

The cruelest torture imaginable.

I watch a poor girl get a belting that would have anyone pleading for mercy, and yet she remains mute. She whimpers, she cries out with each contact of leather against flesh, but she never begs.

I'm helpless. I can't do anything to help her. I want to grab that belt and beat the living shit out of the monster. I want to wrap the leather strap around his neck and suffocate the life right out of him. With every wallop, my desire to kill the man grows. I want him dead. I want to murder another human being. I want to become the monster he is but even worse. I want to make him pay. Pay in the most agonizing way possible.

"Enough!" I shout.

Richard doesn't stop. Instead, he looks at me with an evil grin and snaps the implement on her twice as hard as he had been doing. Ember howls into the musty air of the cellar but does not collapse even though her knees wobble.

"Stop! Stop! You cruel bastard!" I stand from the chair, though I know my actions mean nothing to this man.

His venomous smile grows. His whipping intensifies.

"For the love of God, fucking stop!"

I have to do something. Think. Outsmart. Otherwise he will beat the girl within inches of her life just to prove a point to me and make me suffer.

Ember screams this time as the belt cracks against her, and I nearly vomit.

"She's mine!" I yell, which has him pausing mid swing. "She's my fiancée, and I demand you stop touching her in this way. She's not your concern to discipline in the eyes of God. She's now *mine*!"

My words seem to work because he lowers the belt, and then pulls Ember's dress back over her red and raw ass. He reaches for Ember's midsection and helps her to a standing position.

"You're right," he says, his sinister eyes glaring at me. "This should be *your* duty." He hands Ember the belt. "Ember, go to your future husband, present yourself for punishment, and allow him to finish the task."

She holds the belt in her tiny fist and slowly walks toward me. Her eyes are downcast, which I'm grateful for because I wouldn't be able to look her in the eyes either. I blame myself for her pain and humiliation. I curse myself for not being able to take control of the situation and save her. My body aches far worse than it would had Richard beat me with the belt himself.

"The punishment is over," I try to dictate.

"No," Richard states simply. "Five more lashes before it's complete. Either you do it as your duty, or I'll step in and do it myself. And if I have to, your whipping boy will suffer the consequences for your weakness in being a man."

"I'm sorry," I hear Ember say so quietly I doubt her father hears her. She hands me the belt, turns around, bends over at the waist, and touches her toes.

She is in position.

I have never struck a woman or even so much as desired to.

I glance at Richard and know that if I refuse, he will teach me a lesson with my already sore and trembling *whipping boy*. Fighting back the bile and rage that wants to erupt from my gut, I lift her dress up as I know will be expected of me.

Five. Just five.

I raise the belt and bring it down on her red ass cheek. The weight, the gravity, and my inexperience has me hitting her far harder than I planned. Ember remains stoically quiet, and part of me feels she is doing it for my benefit.

Four. Just four.

"Harder," the sick asshole directs.

Wanting to get this ordeal over with as fast as I can, I bring the belt to her skin again. I feel the contact in my hand, in my soul, and I shatter as I hear a tiny mewl release from her lips.

Three. Just three.

I strike again, and her mewl turns into a sob. I want to hold her. Comfort her. I want to promise her that all will be okay, and I will never let anyone hurt her again.

But I am the one hurting her! Two... just... I can't count anymore. I can barely breathe let alone attempt to cope.

She cries out as I whip her again, and a part of me dies.

I stare directly into Richard's eyes as I deliver the final blow and silently vow to make the man suffer. Revenge will be mine. For Ember.

From this moment on, if there was one thing I would do, it will be to save this woman. Never, never will this woman suffer again while I do nothing to stop it.

I quickly cover her with the fabric of her dress and instinctively pull her into my arms. She needs comfort. I know this. She deserves this.

At first, Ember is stiff, but when I press her head into my chest and gently stroke her hair, she relaxes in my hold. I bring my lips to her ear and whisper, "I will never allow that to happen again. Never."

I know Richard is watching. I know he's considering if he is all right with this unexpected and surprising act of affection—even to me—but I don't care. He will have to come to where we stand to pull Ember away, and I'll kill him with my bare hands before I'll let her go back to him.

"It's not easy being the head of the household," he says as he leans against the doorframe showing he has no intent to stop me from holding his daughter, nor does he plan to leave the cellar.

I have nothing to say in response because I feel I have nothing left inside of me. I can only concentrate on the trembling girl who now clings to my shirt in a silent desperation for more.

More what?

What can I offer?

I have no answers.

Richard won this battle in this war of mine. He decimated his enemy leaving me in nothing but shattered pieces. If this was his intent, then he succeeded.

"Ember is a good girl. I hope she doesn't have to suffer again," he says. "I'm going to go back to work and will be home in plenty of time for an early supper. Ember..."

She lifts her head from my chest and turns to face him. "Yes, Papa Rich?"

"You be a good girl, you hear?"

"Yes, Papa Rich." Her voice is so soft. Delicate. Not an ounce of hate or disgust. How can she remain almost angelic in response when the man just... how the fuck does she do it?

He leaves, and for the first time since he arrived, I feel like I can fully breathe. I still hold Ember and neither one of us seem to want to pull away. I think if we do, it means we have to face what happened and neither of us are ready for that moment. I don't want to have to look her in the eyes. I don't want to have to see my reflection which I can only imagine appears like a monster.

"I don't blame you," she mumbles against my

chest as she seems to press herself even closer. "I know that wasn't easy for you."

If this had been an hour ago, I would be pushing her to help me escape. Demanding that she see the man she calls Papa Rich as the fucking sick perverted man he is. Frustration would be growing in me at her lack of action. I would want to strangle her for not seeing the way I did.

But not now.

Now, I understand. I get it.

I will never blame Ember again. I will never expect this broken child trapped in a woman's body to be whole. She's splintered, and I can see that. I can feel that. All it took was one taste of the man's poison for me to fall into her deep and dark hole myself.

I understand.

"I'm so sorry, Ember."

I close my eyes and inhale deeply. I smell strawberries.

I kiss the top of her head and squeeze her tighter; not for her but for me. I can't think. I can't plan. I can't plot a way out. All I can do is smell strawberries in the wisps of her blonde hair.

CONVICTION.

Papa's conviction is thick like blood. I can see he has no intention of letting Christopher ever leave Hallelujah Junction. And though I know that fact to be true, I still have no idea what he has planned for us. When do we get married? What happens once we are? I have so many questions but no answers.

I want to ask him. I should be able to ask him. I'm his daughter, and yet I fear him now. He's not the same. Or maybe I'm not. Maybe I'm seeing him through Christopher's eyes rather than my own.

If Papa Rich knew the thoughts I have been thinking...

He can never know. Never.

But today I choose happiness. I stir the batter of the cake I have been wanting to make for

Christopher since day one and focus on joy. I use the last of our sugar and flour, but I know Papa is going into town for supplies today and I added them to the shopping list. I don't always get everything I want, but if I don't ask, then I have no chance of getting. Usually Papa is willing to give me the essentials for baking, but not always.

"Now what do I see here?" I hear the question behind me, and I instantly tense and breathe from my nose. I don't want to smell him. I don't want to see him. I don't want Scarecrow here.

But he's here. It's been four days since his last visit, but I shouldn't be surprised. He always has Papa Rich get supplies from town for him.

"I'm baking a cake," I say, not breaking from stirring in hopes that he sees I'm busy and leaves me alone.

He hobbles to where I'm at, by the sink, and leers over my shoulder at the bowl of batter. No matter how hard I try not to, I smell feces. Scarecrow is dirtier than normal, and his stench is overwhelming. Without warning, he dips his filthy finger into the batter and puts it into his mouth.

"What a treat," he says as he licks his finger clean of the raw cake. "Who's the cake for?" His hand is crusty, scaly in brown and yellow flakes.

My heart sinks as my stomach churns. No way can I serve Christopher this cake now. It's contaminated with the touch of Scarecrow. I'd rather feed Christopher poison than to feed him the disgusting grime of the man standing inches from me.

The cake is ruined.

"For you," I lie. "To thank you for agreeing to marry Christopher and me."

In the corner of my eye, I see Scarecrow beam a toothless and decayed smile.

"For *me*?" His voice is pitched higher than normal. "I've never had a cake made just for me." He leans closer to the bowl and inhales. "My very own cake."

I can't stand the air I breathe for another second, so I walk across the room with the cake batter and make it appear like I'm looking for some ingredient in a nearby cabinet. I've yet to look Scarecrow in the eyes, and I hope to keep it that way. My hope is he will leave due to my lack of engagement.

"I'll have it ready for you when Papa Rich comes back with your supplies this afternoon," I say, trying not to grieve what should have been Christopher's cake.

"Where's your pa now?"

"Down the hill. I think he's waiting for you there." I don't know that he is, but I decide to lie again in hopes that Scarecrow will leave to find him.

I hear the sound of his crutch hitting the

wooden floor behind me as he walks to the door. "I'll go find him. And... Ember..."

I know I have to turn to face him. He's waiting. "Yes?" I say as I spin around and offer a weak smile.

"You'd make a mighty fine wife. If ever this man in the cellar doesn't work out, I plan to make good by you. If need be."

I give a slight nod, and go back to the cabinet, moving spices around in my fake attempt of being busy.

I hear him leave and release the breath I had been holding. I quickly finish the spoiled cake and put it in the oven. I may not be able to offer it to Christopher as planned, but I still have the flowers I picked earlier to try to lighten up his gloomy space. Maybe the little bit of color will cheer him up some.

As I enter the cellar, I see Christopher awkwardly leaned back in his chair, attempting to use his belt buckle to cast a shining light through the window across the room from him. He doesn't even try to hide what he's doing from me.

"I wish you wouldn't do that," I say as I place the mason jar full of jasmine next to where he sits.

He doesn't stop but instead focuses on aiming the shimmering light toward the window.

"No one is out there that can see it," I inform. "And if Papa Rich sees you doing this..."

He stops and stares at me, then at the flowers.

"And what am I supposed to do?" he asks. "It's been days. Days!" He raises his voice, but I'm not afraid of him. I can feel his anger is not directed at me.

He's frustrated, and I don't blame him. Caged animals want to be free.

I point to the flowers. "I picked the last of the jasmine for you. The first snowfall is coming soon, and things will change."

"How?" he asks as he repositions himself on the chair, giving up on his attempt of escape by belt buckle.

"You haven't angered Papa Rich since... well since last time. And everything gets better here when it snows. The tourists leave, the town is closed, and the road here becomes impossible to travel without a truck and chains, and even then, it's difficult."

"How is that better?"

I glance down at the chain on his ankle. "I think I can eventually convince Papa Rich to remove the chain. To allow us to move freely in the other buildings. Maybe you and I can stay someplace besides the cellar. Maybe the schoolhouse can become our home... after we're married." I feel my heart flutter and my mouth dries. "Papa Rich is less strict in the winter. And well... I choose to have hope the upcoming snow storm means good for you... for us."

Christopher smirks. "I seriously doubt he'll

ever take this chain off. I'd run, and he knows it. And if I could get close enough to him, I'd kill him. He knows that too. I'd do whatever I could to escape this hell."

"You can't run in the winter. It's impossible."

"How so?"

I point as his bare feet and then at mine as I wiggle my toes. "There's a reason we don't have shoes. I've never worn a pair of shoes in my life except for snow boots when I'm allowed to go snowshoeing, but Papa keeps those with him. We'd get frostbite and lose our toes before we'd even make it to the gate. If somehow you made it to the gate, there are cameras and alarms to let Papa Rich know of trespassers. He'd be down the road in his truck before you'd get far. And even after the gate, there are miles of dirt road before reaching the town. No shoes, means no escape."

"Cameras. Gate. Escape. Do you hear yourself? Is this a normal conversation for you? You must see how wrong this is. Your father has kidnapped me. He's holding me here against my will. Surely you see the insanity in this."

"It's just the way it is," I say softly, not necessarily disagreeing with Christopher, but not wanting to agree either. Because if I agree, what does that mean?

Is my Papa Rich the monster that Christopher believes him to be?

He reaches out and takes my hand. His eyes connect with mine and I see sadness. "Ember," he says slowly. "The fact you're telling me all these details means you've thought of running away. It means you know deep down you're a captive here just as much as me. You know this don't you?"

I shake my head. "No. I'm not a captive. I'm just telling you what Papa Rich has told me. He told me that if I ever get curious and want to go to town, that it would be impossible. He was telling me this for my own good. Just in case I wanted to go to the store myself to buy sugar or a book."

Christopher squeezes my hand, but not hard. "You've never had a pair of shoes?"

I shake my head as I look down at his fingers intertwined with mine. I like the connection. I like the feel. His fingers are cold due to the temperature of the room, but mine are warm, and I enjoy knowing I'm heating his with the touch.

"He doesn't allow you to wear shoes, so you won't run," he says.

"It's for my own good. Curiosity killed the cat, right?" I smile in hopes to lessen the tension I'm feeling.

"Don't you ever want to leave Hallelujah Junction?" he asks with the softest of voice. "You've spent your entire life here. Don't you ever want to see what's out there? Wouldn't you like to go to the store yourself? Wouldn't you like to wear a pair of shoes?"

These questions...

I never gave myself the luxury of thinking this way in the past.

If Papa knew we were having this discussion...

"We all have different paths in life," I say as I release Christopher's hand. I need space and walk to the crate that has become my chair as of late.

"And yours is to stay locked up in a schoolhouse forever?"

I don't like this conversation. It makes my heart beat hard and my stomach tighten. I glance to the door and hope that Papa Rich isn't within earshot.

"We need to be good," I nearly whisper. "If we keep being good, Papa Rich will reward us. I know it. He'll give us more freedom. And once he does, you'll see just how special Hallelujah Junction is. I have so many places I want to show you. There are so many secrets here." I give a big smile to him and feel my cheeks heat in excitement for future possibilities of happiness. "I don't believe in ghosts... not really. But at the same time, you can nearly hear them speak in the walls of these buildings. If you listen real close."

"And I have special places I'd like to show you," he says. "But they aren't here. There's so much more than *here*."

Delusion is easy.

Reality is hard.

But I still want to ask the next question.

"If you could leave here, would you really take me with you?"

"Would you be willing to leave with me?" he asks.

Papa Rich had always taught me to answer every question asked of me honestly, but I can't in this case. Because I don't know.

"This is my home," I say because that is the only truth I know.

He nods in understanding. "But this isn't mine."

I criss cross my legs and settle in. I have a bit of time before I have to take Scarecrow's cake out of the oven and start making lunch. I want to spend the time with Christopher and to continue to learn about this man.

"Tell me about your home," I say, hoping he'll open up to me.

He swallows hard but then smiles. "New York is about as polar opposite of this place. It's loud, it's busy, it's full of life and energy and I love it. You can feel the life of others sizzle in your blood."

"I've read about it."

"Words and stories can't give it justice. You really have to live it."

"Do you have a big house there?" I try not to picture Christopher and me living in New York together as husband and wife, but the thoughts force their way into my imagination. The fantasy of what could…

"An apartment. There aren't a lot of houses in the city. I grew up in a fairly large townhouse in the Upper Eastside with my mother, but square footage is usually limited when it comes to living space unless you're really wealthy." He looks at me and smiles again. "You'd like my place. It has a view of Central Park, and at night, the lights of the city truly are magical. I could sit and stare out the window for hours."

"Are you wealthy?" I figure he is because of his conversation with Papa Rich when he first arrived, but I don't know for sure.

He chuckles. "I suppose so. My family has a lot of money. But I do pretty good for myself as a photographer. I never had to work, but I wanted to. It was important for me to earn my own way. To be my own man. I love what I do. My career is very important to me. So much so, that I suppose it consumed me in all ways. I chose work over all else. Passion has a way of doing that." He pauses and then asks, "What about you? Isn't there some sort of career you would want to do? What did you dream of being when you were a little girl?"

Another question I don't have the answer for.

I don't dream of things like this.

I don't dream at all.

Passion is a foreign thing to me. It doesn't exist in my world.

"I like to draw. I like to read." As soon as I say the words, I realize how small and hollow they sound.

"But no dreams of a future?"

He doesn't seem like he's judging me, or even has pity which is what I have felt from him since his arrival. He seems interested, and for the first time, I feel he really wants to know the person I am.

Christopher is easy to read. I think he believes he's not, but his eyes and the way he shifts his jaw reveals all. I've seen his rage, his sadness, his fear, and his acceptance. I've also seen how he views me. He doesn't hate me like he hates Papa Rich, but he's sad for me. His heart breaks for me. I see it all. I feel it all. But today... right now... I feel a different emotion from him.

Curiosity.

He's trying to figure me out. He's trying to understand how I think and what I feel. He wants to know. Not just because of escape possibilities, but for something more.

I can feel it. Christopher is trying to see me as I have been trying to see him.

I shake my head and focus on the ground before me. "I wake up each day and live the now. Dreams can also be nightmares, so I avoid both."

11

CHRISTOPHER

FIVE DAYS.

Five fucking days.

How long am I going to be expected to live in a cellar, chained to a wall? This can't be my life now. This can't be my normal, and yet, I'm starting to realize that my only chance of escape rests with a psychopath and his terrified daughter.

I'm fucked.

I might as well be dead.

Oh yeah... in the eyes of my family and friends, I am dead.

"Good morning," Ember says as she walks into the cellar with a breakfast tray full of eggs, bacon and toast. Her cat is close behind her feet, and I can see such happiness in her eyes. A stark contrast to my despair.

I can't even bring myself to say anything to her

or even bother to get off my pile of blankets I sleep on. Why bother?

She places the tray next to me on the floor and walks over to the small window across the room and looks up. "It's snowing."

Part of me wants to strangle the smile right off her face.

Great… snow. Snow means the tourists will soon stop arriving and any chance of being heard, being seen, or being rescued will be gone forever. Snow suffocates hope.

"Not a big storm yet," she continues. "Papa Rich can't close Hallelujah Junction yet, but soon." She spins on her bare feet to look at me with the same warm smile that hasn't left her face since entering the room. "And when he does, I really think I can convince him to give us some more freedom. You've been good."

"Good?" I say, raising an eyebrow as I do. "What choice do I have in the matter?" I jiggle the chain around my ankle that has nearly rubbed the flesh of my ankle raw. "Not like I can be anything but 'good'."

She crawls up onto the crate she sits on daily, and her cat cuddles up next to her. It's what she does every single day. Every single day of the five days I've been in this hell. It's our routine. It's our life. We sit and talk. She breaks the awkward chit chat by going to make meals. We then sleep. Repeat. Repeat. Fucking repeat!

She points to the untouched breakfast. "Aren't you hungry? Are you not in the mood for eggs?" Worry marks her tiny face. "I can make something else if you want."

I sigh deeply and run my fingers through my hair. It takes everything inside of me not to lose my absolute shit on this poor woman. I go from moments of pure rage, frustration, and fury to pity, sympathy, and even genuine concern. I feel for this girl. As I'm starting to hear more and more about her life here, I can clearly see just how much of a victim she is. She doesn't see it for herself, however, and though I try to get her to see the reality of her situation time and time again, she refuses. Her wall is so high around her feelings toward Richard I realize I may have no chance of ever breaking down the evil foundation that's been built by a madman and his delusions.

"I need a change of clothes," I say. I struggle to keep my voice calm and even gentle because I'm discovering just how easy Ember spooks. "I appreciate being able to clean myself in the bathroom, and the towel you gave me, but I can't keep wearing the same clothing."

I have never been so filthy in my life, which was really saying something considering some of the adventure photoshoots I had been on in my time. I can't smell myself yet, but it's just a matter of time until that happens. Ember had given me soap, a toothbrush and even a comb. But sleeping on the floor in a dirty cellar, not to mention being dragged in here had me covered in grime that's getting worse by the day.

Nibbling the bottom of her lip and circling her blonde hair with her finger, she says, "You're taller and bigger than Papa Rich. Plus, most of his attire is his ranger uniform."

"Am I expected to live here and be your husband in the same clothes forever?"

It's an asshole move to bring up our fucked up impending matrimony with Ember. It instantly makes her jump to action and get me whatever I want. She aims to please, and I know it. Now if only I can figure out how to manipulate her enough to get me out of this place. I want her to jump up and find me a key to my shackles, but I know I have to take baby steps with her if I have any chance at all.

She hops off the crate and rushes to me. "But I have a washer and a dryer upstairs. I can wash your clothes and bring them right back down to you."

I can see how excited she is at the thought of serving me in this way.

Not wasting a moment, I strip off my shirt without the least bit of embarrassment or shame. I don't care if she sees me nude. I've never been ashamed of my body and, considering I had already lost all sense of dignity being chained to a wall like a mangy mutt, I have nothing left to lose.

When Ember sees what I'm doing, her face reddens, and she quickly turns her back to me. "I'm sorry... I..."

"Why are you sorry?" I drop my pants and underwear to my ankles and just stare at her.

I can see she doesn't want to turn around and see me, and the asshole I am, decides it's time to mess with her head some.

"I'm going to be your husband," I say. "You're going to have to see me naked. A lot."

Her body tenses, and she peeks over her shoulder at me. I see her eyes drop down to my dick and then a small gasp escapes her lips.

"I take it you've never seen a penis," I say, already knowing damn well she hasn't. Unless her kidnapping father is more sadistic than I already knew he was.

She shakes her head and turns completely away from me again but reaches her hand out so I can give her the clothing. When I move to completely remove them, I realize there is no way to fully take my pants and underwear off with the chain around my ankle.

"Slight problem," I say, shaking the chain for emphasis. "Unless you have a key, I'm not able to hand these to you."

"Oh no," she says softly as she glances over her

shoulder and looks at the chain. She shakes her head. "I don't have the key, and Papa Rich won't..." Her voice fades away as she studies the chain, glances at my pants, and then back at the chain.

"I guess you won't be doing my laundry after all."

She bites her lip and turns to face me, still staring at the chain as if trying to come up with a solution. Suddenly, her eyes light up. "Hold on, I have an idea." She quickly runs out of the room.

I feel ridiculous standing naked with my pants pooled around my ankles, so I pull them up and actually hate the idea that I may never truly be clean again.

As I get ready to sit in my chair of dignity— filthy—I'm stopped when Ember comes running back into the room with a pair of scissors in her hand.

"I'll cut them along the outside seam and then sew buttons on them so we can take them off you easily from now on. I know how to sew, and I have a jar of buttons upstairs." She pauses and then shrugs. "The buttons won't all match, but I guess it doesn't really matter."

She doesn't wait for me to answer, but instead kneels at my feet and begins cutting along the fabric. I don't stop her, although I'm not sure how having buttons up my entire leg will work, but it's not like I have a lot of options either. At least she's trying, and I have to give her an A for effort.

When she reaches my underwear, she asks, "Do you want me to sew buttons on these too?" I can see her face is bright red. "I mean... do you want to keep them? I don't mind... I just, I just want you to be comfortable."

"Go ahead and cut them off. I can go commando from here on out."

As sick as it is, I struggle to not smile. The poor girl is extremely uncomfortable having to be so close to my privates, and the fact that my clothes are just a few snips away from falling off of me, with her face right in front of my groin area... well, the humor is not lost on me. I grant her some mercy and help her lower my pants off me completely. She tries her best not to look at me, but I also know there is no way she didn't get an eyeful.

"I'll be back as soon as I can," she says as she scurries out of the room with my soiled clothes in hand and doesn't even bother to close the door behind her.

Being trapped must be getting to me, because I actually have to fight back the urge to laugh. The absurdity of my situation. The fact that I'm sitting on wool blankets in a near dungeon being held captive by a lunatic and about to marry a waif of a woman who would kiss my feet if I ask, is

something no one would ever believe. This is a
nightmare I can't wake up from.

Wrapping a blanket around myself, I settle
against the wall, pull the breakfast tray to me, and
begin eating. I notice the slices of oranges on the
plate are perfectly peeled as if Ember had
painstakingly pulled every little piece of pith on
the fruit off. She wants so desperately to be the
good wife she has read about in books or what she
has been told by Richard. I can see how hard she
tries to please in her domestic duties. And yet... I
wonder if I ever have a chance of convincing her to
help us run away. I wish it's easy trying to reason
with her.

But there's no reason in lunacy.

I take a sip of cold coffee and wish for a shot of
whiskey to add to it.

Five days.

Five days with no booze. No pills. No sex. No
life.

The shakes are subsiding with each new
morning, but it makes me realize just how
dependent my body is on my lifestyle. The cravings
make this entire situation even worse. Detoxing in
a twisted medieval horror story is about as bad as it
can get.

Eventually Ember reenters the room with my
clothes folded nicely in her arms almost as fast as
she had left. "I was able to get most the dirt out, I

think. There's a hole in the leg that I can mend later if you want, but since I took so long with the buttons, I didn't want to keep you waiting any longer."

I stand up on full display. Since she's walking toward me, there is no way she can turn her back on me now. I want her to see me. I want her to face me. I want her to see the reality of what is right in front of her.

Bold, bare, and stripped.

Once she sees me, her eyes quickly dart to the floor. Funny how my nudity causes more discomfort in her than seeing me chained to a wall against my will does.

"Thank you," I say, deciding to give her some mercy and get dressed quickly. That and my balls were damn near freezing off with the chill in the room. Although it's not easy pushing the buttons through each hole that run from my ankle to waist.

I notice as I'm dressing that her cat never leaves her side, it follows her around wherever she goes. Instead of walking to her crate, as I expect her to do, Ember moves toward my pile of blankets and begins to fold and position them into a nice little bed again. She then grabs the tray from breakfast and brings it over to the doorway. She then walks to the bathroom, and I can hear the water running as I guess she is cleaning that area the best she can.

Quite the dutiful woman she is.

"What's going on in here?" Richard booms from the doorway. "Sinners!" he seethes.

I spin around and see wide eyes full of hate directed my way. I'm only wearing my pants as I haven't had time to put my shirt on yet due to how long the buttons took on the pants, and I smirk. I know what he's thinking.

Think it, motherfucker.

Imagine me fucking Ember as she cries out my name.

He takes a step into the room as I know he wants to charge toward me and strangle me with his bare hands, but he halts... not a stupid man. He remains in the doorway out of reach.

"Papa Rich..." Ember says, coming out of the bathroom. Her eyes glance at my bare chest, her mouth drops as her lower lip begins to tremble. She knows what he's thinking too.

"Get over here now!" Richard demands. He points to the spot right beside him and as Ember quickly moves to obey, I stop her.

Placing my hand in front of her and pushing her behind me, I say, "No. She'll be staying right where she is."

"Ember, now!" he shouts as spittle spews from his chapped lips and his face reddens.

"I said no," I repeat as I grab Ember by the arm in case she decides to try to make a run for it toward her father. Although, I also assume she isn't thrilled about the idea of being within her father's reach at the moment.

Regardless that I'm enjoying knowing the thought of me having sex or even being inappropriate with Ember is making the man go insane with anger, I also am not going to allow him to whip her again.

"I had to wash his clothes," she tries to explain.

"Ember, you have two seconds to get over here, or I will blister your ass raw."

"Come and get her," I taunt. "Or are you afraid to face me like a man?"

I can feel Ember try to pull away, but I know the man will beat her as I'm forced to watch. No way will I ever allow that to happen again if I can help it. Plus, it feels damn good to have some control over a situation again.

Richard wants Ember.

He can't have her.

An evil grin spreads across Richard's face as he takes a step backwards. "All right... if you two want to be together so much, then fine. Ember, you can stay in here with our guest. It's high time you both get closer anyway since the wedding day is coming."

He quickly turns around, storms out of the room, slams the door shut. The sound of keys on the other side, and then a click tells me all I need to know.

He locked Ember in the cellar with me.

Ember breaks from my hold and runs toward the door and tries to open it to no avail. She bangs on it and screams, "Papa! I'm sorry. I was only doing his wash. I swear! Nothing happened."

His voice comes from the other side of the door. "Pray, Ember. Pray for forgiveness for your sinful ways. God will forgive. And when he does, I'll return. Until then, pray."

"Papa, I didn't sin. I swear! I swear!"

No answer.

"Papa! Please!" She jiggles the handle again, but there's no opening it.

She turns and looks at me wild-eyed. "It's locked. He's gone."

I smirk and open my arms wide. I shouldn't make light of the situation. I shouldn't allow my sick sense of humor to take over. But I can't help myself. "Welcome to my prison, my dear."

THE CHAINS OF SIN STRANGLE MY SOUL. I DIDN'T mean to be this way. I didn't mean to cross the bridge where the Devil sat.

"I'm sorry," I say to Christopher.

"For what? Doing my laundry?"

"For sinning and bringing you down the hole with me."

Christopher finally puts his shirt on and then sits down on the chair looking at me still standing by the door. "You didn't sin."

"I did."

He tilts his head and his eyes narrow. "Because your father told you so? Is that why you think you sinned?"

I make my way to the crate feeling deep shame. "Papa Rich knows. He could see it. Feel it."

"See and feel what?"

"I looked at your... I saw your..." I try to confess but can't say the vile word.

He smirks. "My what?"

He's going to make me say it.

"My what?" he asks again.

"Your manhood," I blurt. "I saw it. I sinned."

Christopher chuckles and shakes his head. "I can't believe you said 'manhood'." He laughs again but then quickly steadies his emotions. "And yes, Ember, you're going to see my *manhood* if we're going to be married. It's not a sin. It's part of life. It's normal. Sex is normal and will be part of our life." He pauses. "Unless you don't want to get married?"

I quickly shake my head, worried that I offended him with my words. "No, that's not it. I want to marry you. I mean... I have to marry you."

"You don't have to marry me if you don't want to. I can help you. I mean it when I say I'll protect you. And if you choose to, we can run away together, and you don't have to marry me or face my *manhood* ever again."

Not wanting to discuss this further and feeling as if my face is several shades of red, I turn my attention to finding my cat.

"Pine Cone," I sing out, looking behind the crates. "It's okay. You can come out."

"Your cat hates your father."

I nod. "She's afraid of him. Always has been."

"What about you?" Christopher asks. "Are you afraid of him?"

I don't want to answer the question, but I have a feeling Christopher will insist that I do.

"Sometimes," I mumble, not seeing Pine Cone but knowing she is most likely in the furthest corner of the room behind the larger crates where I can't reach her.

"Do you think that's normal? For a daughter to fear her father?"

I shrug, really not wanting to discuss this further. "I'm like my cat. I scare easily."

"He locked you in here with a stranger. He was going to whip you again if I didn't stop it, and he did all this for what? You did nothing wrong. Do you feel this was fair or the actions of a good man?"

I give up looking for Pine Cone and instead walk over to the empty breakfast tray that is still by the door. I take a bowl that I used to put the slices of oranges in and make my way to the bathroom. Once there, I fill up the bowl with water and then go put it by the crate I usually sit on with Pine Cone. I want her to have fresh water when she finally gets the courage to come out.

"I hope Papa Rich allows me out soon. I don't want Pine Cone to be hungry. There's no food for her."

"I'm sure there's plenty of mice down here for

her to hunt. She'll be fine," he reassures. "But that doesn't exactly help us."

"He won't let us go hungry. Whenever he gets angry, he calms quickly, "I say, hoping this situation would be like the ones of my past. "He just needs a day or two."

"A day or two?" He shakes his head and then stares at the ceiling as he inhales and exhales loudly. "Ember, I'm finding it really difficult to stay patient with you. I know your heart isn't evil. I know you aren't like him, but at the same time, what you're doing is wrong. Don't you see that? I know you know the difference between right and wrong. I know you do, and you have to be feeling this is wrong. Me being here is wrong."

I sit on the crate and cross my legs. I refuse to answer. I refuse to think about his words. I refuse.

"Your father speaks of sin, but he's the sinner. He's killed people in those acid pits, right?"

Nodding, I admit, "He has. I hate when he does. I hate it so much, but he says God makes him. God gives him permission."

"Do you believe that? Truly believe that?"

"Why would Papa Rich lie?"

"Because he's a bad bad man, and I think you know this, Ember." He points to the area where Pine Cone is hiding. "Your cat knows this." He tilts his head, pauses and then asks a question that feels like a punch to the belly. "Have you seen him kill people?"

I don't want to answer.

"You have, haven't you?"

"He's protecting me," I try to defend. "He says it's only the people who don't follow the no trespassing signs. They're getting too close to me, and if they do and see me, I'm at risk. He's doing it out of love."

"Do you really believe that?" Christopher asks. "Do you agree with that? Do you think the people he's killed deserve it?"

"No," I answer truthfully. "I hate it. I hate it so much." I feel tears burn the back of my eyes. "I've begged him not to. But..."

"He's a sick and demented man, Ember. Deep down you know this."

"He makes mistakes," I mumble. "But all humans do. It's the nature of man."

Christopher extends his arms and motions around him. "Is that what this is? A mistake?"

As if Papa Rich can hear us talking about him, the door opens, and he takes one step inside. He has a box of crackers, two apples, and a container that is full of what I know is last night's chicken. He places them by the door and then pulls out a newspaper from his back pocket.

I quickly run toward him and kneel at his feet. I

need to make this right. "I'm sorry, Papa. I'm a sinner and will repent however you deem necessary. I don't want Christopher to have to suffer for my misdeeds."

Kissing the top of his boot, the dust of the Nevada desert coats my lips, but I continue on to kiss his other boot. I steal a glance up and see he's not looking down at me but instead at Christopher.

He tosses the newspaper down to me and says, "Read this to your future husband."

I scramble to my feet and do as he asks. I can see exactly what he wants me to read. It's an article about Christopher and his so-called accident.

I clear my throat and begin.

Christopher Davenport, son of the textile heiress Louisa Davenport, has suffered an accident and is now presumed dead. While on a photoshoot in Nevada, he never returned to his Jeep and was reported missing. After conducting an investigation, it was determined he suffered a tragic and fatal accident and fell to his death while trying to capture pictures for an article he was working on about the mysterious ghost town of Hallelujah Junction.

I pause and look at Christopher, my heart breaking for him as he is forced to sit and listen to this. He's pale and his mouth is slack in what I can only assume is disbelief.

"Keep going," Papa Rich demands.

My hands shake as I hold the paper, but I do as I'm asked.

Mr. Davenport isn't the first to suffer such a tragedy in Hallelujah Junction. When the ranger who oversees the historical landmark of a town was asked to comment, he said, "We've had this happen several times in the past. We post warning signs and no trespassing signs to warn of the dangers, but some curious tourists take the risk anyway. The mining pits and old tunnels are extremely dangerous around here. There are acid, toxic gases, hidden shafts, and other lethal elements that make this area deadly if you're not careful. It's a shame he thought a picture was more valuable than his safety and ultimately his life."

Christopher was a well-known photographer for Rolling Stone Magazine *and also had many prestigious photo credits in* National Geographic *and other adventure magazines. His funeral services will be held at St. Joseph Presbyterian Church on November 2nd. The family asks that you respect their privacy during this difficult time.*

I fold the newspaper as I say the last word, and I don't want to see Christopher's face. I know I will see pain. I will see heartache, and I'm not sure I can handle it.

"You sick son of a bitch," Christopher says as he stands from his chair and walks toward us like an animal stalking his prey. He's slow, each step is deliberate and the hatred in his eyes takes my breath away.

Papa Rich remains in the doorway unfazed and

crosses his arms smugly. "I told you. I knew it was just as simple as telling them that you are just another careless victim of the acid pits. Bones and flesh sizzled to nothing. No way to know really, but what else could have possibly happened?"

Christopher makes his way to where we stand and extends the chain as far as he can but it's not long enough. "I dare you to enter this room," he nearly hisses. "Face me. Rather than standing in the doorway like the coward you are, face me. Face me!"

Papa Rich doesn't move. He doesn't seem angry or frightened in the slightest. "They were here. Feet from that window." He points to the narrow cellar window. "They searched high and low for any sign of you. Sadly, they found your camera near the pits. Boot marks with your shoe size near unstable beams that were broken from a heavy weight. Sad. Sad. Sad." He shakes his head in mock mournfulness. "Such a shame. If only he followed the rules or the posted signs."

"Not everyone in my life is going to believe that," Christopher says. "More will come. They'll find me, and when they do, I'll kill you with my bare hands."

Papa Rich shrugs. "Your mother is quite the entitled bitch. She had the nerve to call me and demand to know how this 'incompetence' can occur. She even threatened to sue the State

Forestry Department for the unsafe conditions of the town. Not that I care really. Not my problem. Other than the fact I've been asked to post more signs and to gate off the old mill. Not that it will help any. The curious tourists will still come... and they will still die."

Christopher screams in frustration and yanks the chain around his ankle as hard as he can. And for a split moment I wonder if he'll be able to break free with all the pent-up rage inside of him.

"Ember, your fiancé is upset. Which is understandable. It's not easy to hear about your own death." He pushes me toward Christopher. "Comfort your man. Ease his pain as a good wife would do."

My heart skips because I don't know what he means. Of course I will love if there is a way to comfort Christopher, but I don't know how. I don't want to disappoint Papa Rich in not following his order, but I also fear whatever I do will be wrong.

"Kiss him," Papa Rich commands.

"Fuck you," Christopher spats. He turns and makes his way back to the chair. "Sick motherfucker. Chicken shit."

Papa only continues, "Go to him, Ember. Kiss him and offer comfort."

I've never kissed anyone before. I don't know what to do. I can't. How?

My thoughts must be written on my face

because Papa Rich says, "Unless you want me to take away this food and not come back for days, you will do as I say. Kiss him and I'll be back in one day's time." I see him look at Christopher who is now standing by his chair. "Kiss my daughter or you both will starve down here."

Christopher spins on his heels and his face is bright red as his eyes seem to bulge from their sockets. "What is wrong with you? You are completely insane. Insane! And I swear to your fucked up God that I will kill you someday. I will fucking kill you."

Papa Rich inhales and very calmly says on exhale, "Kiss. Now."

I know that he doesn't like to repeat himself, and he's already done so more than I've ever heard him do. So, not wasting any more time, I pad across the cold floor to Christopher and stand before him. I look up into his eyes and silently beg for him to listen and comply. Papa will starve us. I have no doubt in this if we don't listen.

I stand up on my tiptoes and place my hand on Christopher's chest to steady myself.

"Please kiss me," I whisper, hoping only he can hear my plea.

Christopher places his hand on the back of my head and lowers his head to mine. Our lips make contact, and I wonder if he's stealing all my air because I can't breathe. My legs feel weak, my heart beats hard, and my stomach flips.

He smells like the soap I gave him, but also something else—earth and spice. I can feel the heat from his body, and his palm on the back of my head seems to nearly scorch my skin. The hair on his face that has grown since arriving pricks my skin, but the roughness sends a shiver to my toes.

My eyes are closed in fear of what I'll see. I don't want Christopher to hate me. I don't want him to be disgusted. I don't want him to think I'm evil. I just want to block it all out and focus on what's happening.

My very first kiss.

My very first intimate touch of any kind.

My very first time feeling... I don't know what I feel.

Is this the Devil that tingles inside of me?

Is this sin that makes me not want to stop?

Good Lord show me the way.

Is this kiss opening the door to evil and will cease any salvation?

My very first kiss...

The sound of the door closing broke the spell of seduction. We both pull away and look at the door as we hear the key locking us inside.

I touch my lips as I step away from Christopher, embarrassed and ashamed by just how much I like the kiss.

Christopher doesn't say anything but sits in the chair and places his head between his legs. His eyes are closed tightly, and I see such a deep sorrow that I struggle to ward it off myself. I want to cry the tears for him. I want to howl at God for such injustice and scream out in agony. I want to take his pain. I want it all. I deserve it. Not him.

"Your father just killed me. And you stood and watched as he did so."

He's right.

I watched a monster emerge from my father just now. He enjoyed seeing the pain in Christopher's eyes. He fed off it like a carnivore tearing the flesh from his bones.

My Papa Rich...

Who is my Papa Rich?

13

WE REMAINED IN SILENCE FOR SEVERAL HOURS AFTER the kiss. I sat and stared at the words on the newspaper in disbelief. I had held out hope that no one would believe the ramblings of a madman and truly believe I had fallen to my death.

But they all believe.

They all are mourning my death.

I'm dead.

I'm nothing but an empty coffin being lowered into the ground.

"Would you like some crackers and chicken?" Ember finally asks. "You haven't eaten any today. You must be hungry. The chicken's cold, but I'm sure it won't taste bad."

"Have you ever lost someone? Anyone die in your life?" I ask as I look up to her for the first time in what feels like ages.

She shakes her head. "No."

"It's an awful feeling. The pain is indescribable. My mother, my friends and other family are all suffering right now."

Ember pulls her legs up to her chest on the crate and lowers her dress to cover her ankles and feet. It's getting colder by the hour, and the falling snow outside doesn't help matters. I can't see our breath yet, but I have a feeling it's only a matter of time.

"I know you think I can help you," she says as she pets her cat that finally has crawled up on the crate to join her. "And if I could... and knew it would work... then maybe I would. But I know my father. I know this area. I know our reality. I don't want to see you dead."

"Being dead would be better than this."

"Maybe for you," she says. "But I don't want to feel that indescribable pain you speak of. I know it's selfish, but I don't want you dead. Not for real."

"I'll never be happy here," I say.

"Then I'll lend you some of mine. You can borrow my happiness anytime you'd like."

"And are you really happy, Ember? Truly?"

"Not all the time," she admits as she wraps her arms around her tiny frame. "But I hope that I will always be someday. I'm hopeful. And hope gives me some happiness. Sunshine is within reach."

"Then give me some hope," I say. "I need this

sunshine because the darkness is pretty fucking thick right now. Tell me you'll at least consider helping me escape if there comes an opportunity. Tell me you will at least consider it. Give me hope."

"I don't know that I can do that."

Pressing on, I say, "I promise you, Ember. I promise if you help me out of here, I won't leave you behind. I won't abandon you no matter what. I'll take care of you, I'll keep you safe, and you'll never be left alone. If you can make a promise, then so can I."

"I don't want to be alone anymore," she admits softly.

"You won't be."

She remains quiet but then finally nods. "If there comes a time I can help you, I will. I promise."

And just like that, there is a small spark of light in the dark cave of misery I have thrust myself in. Ember is right. Hope does give some happiness. She at least lends me a small grain of sand of hope, and that little bit allows me to breathe again.

"But I know my father," she adds. "He plans everything out. He doesn't make mistakes. And he's determined..." Glancing up and out the window at the falling snow, she moves a piece of her golden hair from her face. Her profile is quite striking in a raw and natural way. "I'm sorry, Christopher. I wish I were stronger. I often wish this, and if I could..."

She turns to stare at me, her wide blue eyes are glassed over in pain. "I wish I could save you."

"Come over here," I say as I watch how she shivers beneath the thin fabric she wears. "Come sit by me in the blankets. I can see you're cold."

"That's your bed," she says, but I can see she's eyeing the blankets.

"It's going to be *our* bed for the time being." I pat the pile of faded wool blankets and settle in to make room. "It's cold in here, and it's only going to get colder."

"My cat might follow me," she says as she hops off the crate. "If that's okay."

"I think we'll need all the heat we can get." I glance at the window and see the snow isn't letting up in the slightest. "Your father doesn't care that you could freeze down here?"

"Penance," she says more to herself than me.

I can see she's uncomfortable approaching me. "I don't bite. Come on, let's get warm."

I adjust the blankets so we have one to sit on, one to wrap around our bodies and then use the third one for our laps while we remain sitting. When we sleep, we'll have to make do with piling two blankets on us and hope it's enough to get us through the night.

Ember kneels down beside me, but I can feel her awkward discomfort.

"I'm not going to hurt you," I say as I move

toward her and wrap a blanket around her, pulling her to my side.

She snuggles up closer to me. "I don't think you will."

"Then why do you seem afraid?"

"I think that's just how I am."

"Afraid?"

"Yes. In one way or the other. Fear is always knocking on my door I suppose."

"That's sad." I secure the blankets around us and actually find a sense of comfort having her next to me.

Maybe fear is knocking on my door as well.

"I know you pity me. I wish you wouldn't." Her voice is soft, not angry, not even sad. Just soft.

"I can't help it," I admit honestly. "I see your truth and reality, and I see a nightmare. And what I pity is you can't see it for yourself. You're a victim and too blinded by that fear you speak of to know it."

"Papa Rich loves me."

"Maybe so. I won't argue that. Although at the same time, why would a man who loves you lock you up in a cold cellar with a complete stranger chained to the wall? How does he know I won't harm you in retaliation? How does he know if you'll be all right? Wouldn't a father be concerned if his daughter is cold at the very least?"

"He's a strict man."

Ember keeps her eyes focused straight ahead, but I'm a little surprised she isn't trying to pull away or give some space between us. Our bodies are pressed snugly together, and though she is tense, she is remaining close. I don't want to keep pressing her on her father because I could end up pushing her away, so I decide it's best to change the subject if possible. Although there is another part of me that still wants to shake some sense into this girl. A violent urge to grab her by the throat and strangle her just to teach Richard a lesson. Just to hurt him as he's trying to hurt me. To make him pay for his lunacy.

If I kill Ember—which would be so easy to do right now—would I destroy the man as I so desperately want to do?

But does she deserve to die?

Is this her fault?

Taking a deep breath and trying not to let the dark thoughts take over, I say, "I'm sorry about the kiss."

"Sorry?" Ember turns her head to look at me, her beautiful eyes being the only thing I could see.

"You deserve better. Your first kiss should have been so much better. I'm assuming it was your first kiss, right?"

She nods and turns her attention straight ahead. "It was. And it was nothing you should apologize for. I... I liked it," she confesses as she looks down at her fingers which grip the wool blanket. "Is that bad to admit?"

Christ. This woman is as pure and genuine as an innocent child. It's hard to see her as a grown woman. Nothing in life has turned her into a broken and shielded person who would never admit or allow herself to be so vulnerable. I have never had a woman state so simply that she liked a kiss from me. That would make her weak and give me the upper hand.

New York dating laws 101. Don't reveal your true feelings.

"No, it's not bad to admit."

"I've always fantasized about my first kiss. It was nice." I see a smile paint her face and her cheeks pinken.

"Your first kiss should not have happened by force," I say as I reach for a piece of her hair that is hanging in front of her face and tuck it behind her ear. "When you have memories of your first kiss, your father should not be in the picture."

She shrugs, but her smile fades as she does so. A shiver runs through her and spreads to me. Sitting up against the cold wall isn't going to keep us warm for long, and I know I have to make a change.

"Let's lie down," I say.

She doesn't resist and lies down in front of me on her side. I position the blankets so they will be on top of us and spoon her from behind. Her frame is so tiny I worry the weight of my arm over her will be too heavy.

"Are you comfortable?" I adjust my body until I'm as close to her as I can get and try not to focus on the fact her body is curved against mine and we fit like a perfect glove.

Nothing about this situation is perfect, and yet, Ember's body is warm, and I feel a sense of comfort I haven't felt since being hit over the head by a madman. I also feel this overwhelming need to protect. I like knowing Ember is safe in my arms and no harm can come to her.

I don't want to let her go.

For Christ's sake... why don't I want to let her go?

My eyes dart back to the window. "Ember? Tell me about where we are right now. Where in the town are we?"

"Up the hill from the main street. The ranger's house is hidden by the schoolhouse so the public can't see it. It was designed that way to not alter the ambiance of stepping back in time. They didn't want to see lights on or signs of life from the main area. You were walking toward the house when—"

"What are the chances of someone walking by that window?"

"Rare. And if someone does... it won't end well."

"Because of your father? He'll kill them?"

"Yes, in the acid pits at the mill. You were lucky to not be dead."

I nearly laugh. I am far from lucky right now.

"What about the key to my chain? Do you know where that is?"

She shakes her head and her body tenses against me. I may be pushing too far, but I need to try.

"What about a cell phone? A phone of any kind? Is there a way you can get to a phone once he lets you free?"

"We don't have a phone. There's a ranger's radio, but Papa Rich keeps that with him."

My mind runs wild with ways of escape now that I have Ember—even faintly—open to answering my questions.

"What about that man who was upstairs on the first day? You said he wouldn't help, but who is he? Maybe he would."

Ember shivers and I pull the blanket higher over her shoulder. "Scarecrow. He's a bad man. He won't help. Trust me."

"Scarecrow? His name is Scarecrow?"

"He's missing a leg. Instead of getting a fake one or just doing without, he stuffs his pant leg with straw. He lives further up in the hills by himself. A disgusting hermit who only comes to Hallelujah Junction to visit us. He's vile. He stinks. He's an awful, awful man. And he's also Papa Rich's best friend. If he had his way, he'd be marrying me instead of you. So, if anything, he'd just throw you in the pits himself so he can have you out of the way."

"And you never see anyone?" I continue, not wanting to give up. There has to be someone. Some way...

"Just from afar. I watch the tourists down below. That's it."

"And you said that there are underground tunnels, right? Your father allows you to walk them from building to building?"

"Right."

Okay... this will be a long game.

A fucking twisted and fucked up game.

I will have to play it. I will have to play along so I'm given that moment... the brief moment... to find my opportunity of escape. But it will happen. Not by force, but by wits.

"And when I marry you..." I say as I inhale the strawberry essence from her hair, "you believe your father will let us live freely as you once did?"

"I hope so. I know he has a plan, and I'm sure you and I being able to live a normal life as husband and wife will be part of it." She inhales deeply and then lets it out slowly. "I really hope so."

We lie in silence as I hold her and scan the

room looking for anything to give me an idea of escape. I stare at the window and pray to see boots walking by. I eventually settle in and know I have to think bigger picture. The cat finally joins us and cuddles up against my leg for warmth. I can see my breath now, but I at least feel warm next to Ember.

She's putting off heat in this cold hell.

"Thank you, Christopher," she says as she presses her body even closer to mine. "I know you want to hate me. So, thank you for fighting that emotion off."

"I don't hate you."

"But you have to fight for that. So, thank you."

"Wake up. It's your wedding day." Papa Rich's voice bellows off the cold, dank floor and walls.

I shoot up from the ground and stand as quickly as I can. I pray that Papa doesn't consider my sleeping with Christopher under the blankets in such close proximity as a sin. But I had no choice. If it weren't for Christopher's kindness and sharing the blankets, I'm not sure I could have made it through the night. Even with the wool over me and the heat off of Christopher's body, I still remained cold and uncomfortable for most of the night.

Christopher is much slower in getting off the ground, but he does reach out and grab my arm, no doubt refusing for me to be able to run toward Papa and be within his reach. Although I will gladly take another whipping with his belt over spending another night in the cold cellar.

Papa Rich glances down at the untouched food he sent. We had been too cold to go eat once we found the smallest amount of warmth with our body heat.

"You didn't eat." He looks at me, and adds, "Go make some breakfast for you and your fiancé and make quick work of it. Scarecrow has blessed us with his presence before the next big storm. We think winter's coming fast and furious this year, and he wants to preside over your wedding before it becomes impossible for him to make his way here."

"Today? You want me to get married today?" The words didn't seem real.

"Snow-covered ground, eagles flying overhead in search of prey, and the good Lord's grace deeming it so. What better a day to wed?"

I glance at Christopher, not sure what I will see on his face. Will he storm to Papa Rich in rage again?

"If the Lord deems it so," Christopher says as he shakes out the blankets and folds them nicely and... in such control.

Papa's brow raises and a smile masters his face. "Well lookee here. Isolation has chased the Devil right out of your body." He looks at me and his smile grows even move. "Go on, girl. Get busy. You have to get dressed and ready for your big day, and we don't have a lot of time. Scarecrow wants to head on home before it storms again."

My head spins in uncertainty and confusion. Chaos bangs destruction inside of me. Both men seem... off. Both are unusually happy and at ease when they were both nearly homicidal only hours ago. But at the same time, I'm not going to risk upsetting either, so I quickly run out of the room toward the kitchen with Pine Cone underfoot. And Papa is right... I don't have a lot of time because the smell of onion and sweat tells me that Scarecrow is here and waiting.

When I enter my room after making and serving Christopher breakfast, I am surprised to see a white lace dress spread on my bed. It's not new, and actually quite old based on the discoloration, but it's still beautiful. Long sleeves, delicate buttons that go up the back to the high collar, and such intricate design in the lace fills me with an excitement I have never felt in my life. I've never worn anything so pretty and worth so much money before. I've never received a gift, and for my first one to be so beautiful...

"Do you like it?" Papa Rich asks from behind me.

I pick up the dress and hold it against me. "Where did you find it? It's beyond anything... Oh, Papa Rich." I spin and face him, not being able to control the tears that fall from my eyes. "Thank you. It's perfect."

"My daughter only gets one wedding day."

There's kindness in his eyes. I see it. For the first time since Christopher arrived, I see a small glimmer of my Papa Rich. He's not a bad man... not always. Not always.

He approaches me and reaches into his pocket as he does. "I got these for the both of you too." He pulls out two gold bands and places them in my palm. "Something for you both to wear forever symbolizing your love and unity. And hopefully"—he looks down at his feet and fidgets for a moment—"you remember just how much I love you when you look at it on your finger. I know I have a hard time showing it. I know I'm broken down to the bone, and though I've tried so hard not to show you just how jagged my spirit is, I know you've seen. You're a wise woman. Extremely wise. You see with eyes of a woman far older and experienced than your years. You see me... and for that, I'm often disappointed."

I don't know what to say, but the tears continue to fall. I love him. Christopher may not understand why, and I get that. But right now. This very moment. I love my father. I can't control my heart. I can't control my feelings. And though I should... I can't help but slip back into time and remember that little girl who was so desperate for love and security.

Papa Rich gave me that.

He saved me.

He loved me.

He kept me.

"You deserve the best," he says as he steps away from me and gives me the space I need to process. "True love does not find you. You have to find it. You have to fight for it. And though your nature is not one of a fighter, it's time you learn how. You will have to have an inner strength to be married and to hold that love near at whatever cost."

I look down at the gold in my palm and picture the rings on my and Christopher's fingers. The weight of the bands are heavy with hidden tales of my future. They nearly burn.

What is ahead for us?

Once we become husband and wife... then what?

"You go on and get ready, and then I'll help you with those buttons on the back of your dress," he says. "We don't want to keep Scarecrow waiting long. A storm's brewing and we don't want him getting caught up in it."

He leaves my room, and the sense of warmth I briefly felt is suddenly replaced with a deep chill that runs up my spine. But I do exactly as he commands and dress for my wedding.

THERE'S A CHAIN AROUND MY ANKLE.

There's a chain around Ember's ankle.

We are connected by this chain.

And we are about to be wedded standing before a one-legged pastor who leans on a crutch. The sound of hay rustles beneath his denim pants with the slightest move, and I think it's fair to say I have never seen a more disgusting creature in my life.

I have officially entered a new phase of Hell.

"Good Lord, bless us on this day," the pastor known as Scarecrow begins. "Brother Christopher and Sister Ember stand before the Almighty to be crowned under the union of matrimony."

He looks at Richard who is actually wearing something besides a ranger uniform, although his faded black pants and wrinkled black shirt are far from what I consider fancy.

"Who gives away this woman?" Scarecrow asks.

"I do with the blessing of God. Her father."

Scarecrow raises his arms up toward the ceiling of the schoolhouse, and I see the sweat stains under his pits. His stench nearly makes me as sick as the act of being forced to marry a woman while literally chained to her. This is my wedding day. No guests other than a madman father, no flowers, no best man or bridesmaids. It's my wedding day and I wear the same dirty outfit I arrived in—minus the shoes.

Ember, however, is beautiful in a haunted, captivating way. Her long hair hangs down her back and shines beneath the sunlight that invades the room we stand in. The dress she wears is ancient in appearance but still seems to fit her personality and size perfectly. I feel as if I have stepped back in time, trapped in a bleak and dark vortex, yet Ember does offer some light. The blue in her eyes sparkle with happiness.

My heart breaks over her happiness.

She's happy even though she's chained to me.

She's happy to be marrying me even though it's not by her choice.

She's happy...

We stand inside her favorite place. The

schoolhouse is our church for this day. At least getting here allowed me to see the underground tunnels Ember told me about. Getting outside the cellar allowed me to take mental notes on every step of the way. Richard was smart, however, which I expected him to be. When he showed up with a pistol in his hand and another chain in his hand, I knew what he planned before he even said a word. Shackling me to Ember would make it next to impossible to run unless we somehow mastered running together in a cadence and step that would take careful practice and discussion.

"Now you will feel no rain, for each of you will be shelter for the other. Now you will feel no cold, for each of you will be warmth to the other. Now there will be no loneliness, for each of you will be companion to the other. Now you are two persons, but there is only one life before you. May beauty surround you both in the journey ahead and through all the years. May happiness be your companion and your days together be good and long upon the earth. May you both walk under God as dutiful servants. We honor fire and ask that our union be warm and glowing with love in our hearts. We honor wind and ask that we sail through life safe and calm as in our father's arms. We honor water to clean and soothe our relationship—that it may never thirst for love.

With all the forces of the universe you created, we pray for harmony as we grow forever young together. Amen."

Ember and Richard both say, "Amen," but I can't bring myself to speak.

Scarecrow nearly chants the words, and they sound more satanic than holy. And now it dawns on me why when you see pictures from old backwoods weddings in the Appalachian Mountains or some other small town, the people never smiled. They stood side by side with the look of death on their faces. Dark circles under their eyes and sunken cheekbones.

This is me. I'm the ghostly man in these pictures. I completely understand.

If someone could take a picture of me now, what would they see?

I'm trying to tell myself this is not real. This is an act. This is all a game so I can win in the end.

I'm not really getting married.

This Scarecrow man can't be a real pastor, and even if he is... this isn't real. I'm chained to my bride. I'm fucking chained.

I'm not really holding the hand of my bride— soon to be my wife.

This isn't real.

Scarecrow opens his dirty hands before us, and resting in his palm are two gold bands. I take the smaller one, and Ember takes the larger.

Oh Jesus, this is getting more real by the second. Wedding bands. Something for me to wear every single day. Will it choke the life out of me?

I'm fucking getting married!

"Brother Christopher," Scarecrow breaks my thoughts. "Do you take Sister Ember to be your bride, to honor, to cherish, and to walk under God's eyes together as one?"

"I do," I somehow say as I slide the ring onto Ember's finger.

I have to. I have to stay focused on the plan. The only way to escape is to marry her. At least in this fucked up world I'm locked in.

"Sister Ember." Scarecrow has spittle spewing from his chapped lips, and I force myself to look at the woman before me which is a far better sight. "Do you take Brother Christopher to be your husband, to honor, obey, and walk under God's eyes together as one?"

"I do," she says softly as her eyes connect with mine. She wants this so badly. I can see it in the way her face nearly beams like an angel. I can feel it.

The band slides on my finger and actually fits perfectly even though I wonder if it will blister my skin with the evil it's laced with.

"I now pronounce you husband and wife. You may kiss your bride."

I actually *have* to kiss her. It's the only thing to

keep me standing as my entire being is swirling in complete chaos. I need a grounding force, and the lips of this sweet and pure woman before me are all I have to cling to.

As gently, and as lovingly as I can muster, I bring my lips to hers. She deserves a wedding kiss to remember. She deserves a memory that isn't blanketed in thick darkness. I want to give her that gift. I want her to look back on this moment and remember how happy I truly believe she is.

My lips touch hers and I feel her release a breath. I inhale in hopes that her innocent view on life will help me chase away the horror flowing through my veins. I need her strength. I need her optimism. Otherwise, I'll be swallowed up whole just as if I had been thrown in the acid pits.

"Ember Davenport," Scarecrow says. "Christopher Davenport." His words break our kiss. "You are now joined as one under God."

As I look upon this delicate flower, I want to make my own wedding vows to her.

I want to promise her we will find a way to leave this Hell.

I want to make a vow that she will never have to live this existence again.

I want to offer my words for a future that will be better, safer, and normal.

On this land, in Hallelujah Junction and in the

eyes of all who stand and look upon me, Ember is my wife.

She is my captive bride.

16

I DREAMED OF THIS DAY.

When hopelessness surrounded me, that my existence would be nothing more than being the ghost of Hallelujah Junction, I had dreamed of a Prince Charming arriving from afar who would kiss away all the bad and bring me only good.

I stand before my Prince Charming.

My husband.

I know this isn't what he wants. I know he wants to be free. I know he wants my father dead. But I also know fate has brought him here for a reason. Maybe he simply doesn't know it yet. Maybe it's my job to show him.

I know I can make him happy if I work really hard.

I know I can give him love and tenderness.

I can be a good wife. I know I can. I just have to convince him of that fact.

Papa Rich and Scarecrow leave us alone in the schoolhouse. The act alone shows that the marriage changes things. We aren't going to have to spend our wedding night in the cold cellar. Papa Rich only had one dictate, and one that I am prepared to follow.

"You will lay this white sheet beneath you as you consummate the marriage. God will expect to see the signs of the union."

He wanted proof of Christopher taking my virginity.

But I will do that. I will do anything if it means Christopher can remain in my private sanctuary.

Christopher and I hadn't exchanged any words since our vows, but now that we stand in the schoolhouse alone, I feel it's my duty to break the ice. "This is where I spend most of my time. I have a room in the main house, but I still prefer this place." I point to the windows. "There's a lot of sunshine." I point to the old wood-burning stove. "And we can use this to heat the place in the winter. Not while there are tourists or they'll see the smoke, but we can soon when the tourists leave."

Christopher slowly meanders to the window that overlooks the town. The same window I was at when I watched Papa Rich hit him upside the head.

Because of the chain, I have no choice but to go with him.

"The ghost of Hallelujah Junction." He smirks and then looks at me. "Is now my wife."

My face heats and I look down at the floor at my bare feet. They are dirtier than I like, but I haven't been able to keep up on the cleaning of the floors since I was in the cellar and I was busy with Christopher even before that.

He refocuses his attention outside the window. "When I took this assignment, to capture the sights of the ghost town known as Hallelujah Junction, I actually worried it would be too boring. I almost declined the job. I mean, who cares about an old mining town anyway? Who would read about that, and who would want to look at pictures of run-down dilapidated buildings? Boring." He laughs more to himself than anything. "If I only knew."

We stand there in silence, and I have no idea what to say. I know he's in pain. I know he's sad and angry. I want to make it better. I want to make it all go away.

"I don't know how to be a wife," I confess, feeling like I have to be honest.

He chuckles, still looking outside. "Oh, I can pretty much guarantee I have no idea how to be a husband either."

I swallow against the lump in my throat and glance over my shoulder at the mattress on the floor with the bedding piled on top of it. The white sheet on top of the other blankets brings me back to the reality of what's going to occur soon.

He's going to take my virginity.

"Papa Rich said that tonight is going to hurt."

Christopher turns his head and looks at me with confusion. "What are you talking about? What's going to hurt?"

"When you claim me," I say softly, not being able to look him in the eye as I say the words. "He said it's my duty and that I must just endure the pain. I'm scared," I confess.

"Jesus," he says as he runs his hands through his hair and looks out the window again. "I'm not going to claim you. I would never hurt you, and I sure as hell wouldn't take what isn't given. He can force many things, but he sure as fuck can't force me to have sex with you."

"But we have to consummate the marriage," I say, feeling my heart sink. I don't want to fail at being a wife on day one.

"What he knows or doesn't know is none of his business. We don't have to tell him what we do. Make him believe whatever makes him happy. I don't give a shit."

"Christopher..."

He spins to face me directly. His eyes are filled

with anger. "I'm not going to take your virginity. I'm not that kind of man!" He moves his cuffed leg a little. "I may be chained like a damn animal, but that doesn't mean I'll behave like one."

"You don't want to have sex with me?" My lip trembles as I ask the question, and I struggle to hold back the tears that threaten to fall. I look down at my dress. "Am I not desirable?"

He grasps my chin and forces my head up to look at him. "First of all, you're beautiful. Don't ever feel you aren't. You have a true and genuine beauty I've never seen before in another woman. There's an angelic purity to you that you have somehow maintained even though you live in the absolute pit of despair."

"Then why are you angry?" I ask. "Why is the thought of having sex on our wedding night getting you upset?"

"Because you deserve better!" he snaps. He glances at the mattress on the floor. "Your first experience should be romantic. It should be special. It should be an experience you want and have been looking forward to. I don't want you to have sex because your father demands it."

"But he does," I say, pointing at the white sheet. "He told me he will expect to see proof of it tomorrow morning."

"Motherfucker!" Christopher shouts as he

punches his fist against the wall of the schoolhouse.

I jump back, but I can't fully retreat without falling to the ground as the chain holds one foot in place.

Christopher sees my reaction and instantly softens and pulls me into his arms. "I'm sorry. I'm sorry." He takes a deep breath in. "I don't ever want to scare you."

I pull away just enough so that I can look into his eyes. "Please don't fight him on this. He'll whip me if we refuse, and he'll lock us back in the cellar." I glance around the schoolhouse and add, "I know this may not be your apartment in New York, but it's better than sleeping on the cold floor of the cellar. And I promise I'll try to fix it up real nice. I'll try to make it feel like our home." I glance down at my feet. "Just don't give Papa Rich reason to take it all away. He will. He doesn't bluff."

Christopher lifts my chin so I have to look up at him. "Where I come from, the woman chooses to give her virginity away. It's a gift. And it's not something I'd just take."

"You aren't taking. I'm giving."

"It shouldn't be like this."

"We're husband and wife now. It's what's supposed to be done. And..." My face heats and I divert my eyes in shame. "I'm way past the age. I know this. I shouldn't be a virgin anymore. I don't want to be. I want to be... normal. Or at least as normal as I can be in my setting."

"Your setting?" I see hope in his eyes. I know he wants me to think the way he does. He thinks I live in denial, and maybe I do.

"I know I'm different. I know a normal woman doesn't grow up in a ghost town hidden from the world. I know I'm sheltered." Saying the words out loud actually stabs at my heart. "I'm aware of my circumstances and how they look to you. I also know you *pity* me."

"I wouldn't use the word *pity*," he says. "But I see the truth, and I'm not sure you do."

"What's the truth you see?"

"Your father keeps you here against your will."

I look down at my feet and then back up at him. "You're right. That is my truth."

"Then why don't you want to escape?" he asks.

"It's not a matter of want or not. It's a matter of reality. I know we can't escape. And I also know what the consequences could be. And even if I do escape...if *we* escape. Then what? What do I do? Where do I go? I don't know anyone or anything. I have no idea what is outside of Hallelujah Junction."

"I already told you," he says. "I promised that I would help you. I wouldn't just abandon you."

"And that is *pity*."

"No. That's human decency. I would help you."

"Because you have to? Because we're now husband and wife? Because—"

"Because I'd want to," he interrupts. "I feel this need to protect you, and it's not going to go away just because we leave this town. I promise you that."

He looks over my shoulder at the mattress with the white sheet. His brow furrows, but he doesn't speak anymore. He takes a deep breath, runs his fingers through his hair and then pulls my head against his chest.

"I wish I could rescue you from this place tonight," he says softly. "I wish I could introduce you to a normal life. I wish I could show you life as it's supposed to be. I wish I could give you a romantic wedding night."

I inhale his scent and close my eyes, savoring the fragrance. "You're my husband. Being in your arms, I feel... safe. That's all I need and all I'll ever ask for."

"But you aren't safe. As long as we're here, you'll never be safe."

He's right. I know this deep down. I love my Papa Rich, but I know that one wrong move by Christopher or even me, and his temper could attack. He seems so unhinged, and it's growing deeper and deeper by the day.

I break away from the hold and walk to the mattress. I begin unfolding the sheet and covering the bed with it, taking extra care to smooth out the wrinkles and tuck the corners in snuggly. I want our wedding bed to be as perfect as it can be.

I try to ignore the fear sizzling through my veins. Papa said it would hurt, and he'd never lied to me before, so I believe every word. But I also know it's my duty as a wife, and one that I want to do well. I can't give Christopher true freedom, but I can do whatever I can to make him happy and well cared for. It also shames me that a big part of me is curious and even excited for what's to come. I want another kiss. I want more tender caresses and holding. I want the love. God, how much I want the love.

Not wanting to discuss this further, not wanting to beg for Christopher to comply, and not wanting to wait on anxious breath anymore, I lie on my back and slowly open my legs. I'm not wearing panties because I have none that were fancy enough for such a special day and night.

"I'm ready," I nearly whisper, not sure what else to say. My voice cracks as I say the words.

I stare at the ceiling and wait to hear the slightest noise from Christopher. The first thing I hear is the release of a deep breath and then his footsteps approaching the mattress.

"I can't do this," he says as he towers over me, looking down with sorrow in his eyes. "This isn't me. It feels wrong."

I sit up and reach for his hand. Pulling him down to the mattress, I say, "Please. I know you think it's dark now, but it can get so much darker. We must obey."

"I don't care what he does to me. He can't make me lose who I am to my core."

"He'll hurt me, Christopher," I say softly. "Protect me. As my husband, I'm asking you to please keep me from harm."

I lie back down and close my eyes tightly, preparing myself for what is to come... or at least what I hope is coming.

17

CHRISTOPHER

"Open your eyes," I say firmly. "It won't be like this. I won't have your first time be a memory of you grinning and bearing it because you think it's your wifely duty. If we're going to have sex, then you're going to allow me to make it as special as it can be considering our circumstances."

"Special?" She opens her eyes and looks up at me.

The protective need coursing through me right now is beyond powerful. I don't know why. I don't know why I feel this overwhelming need to give this woman the best that I can, and if that means something as simple as making her first time having sex as pleasant as possible, then so be it.

I position my body so I'm beside her. I look into her eyes and say, "All you have to say is stop, and I will. Ask me to slow down, and I'll listen. Your voice will be heard. Do not suffer through this. Understand?"

She nods and licks her lips as her eyes look at mine.

I lean forward and press my mouth to hers and am surprised when she willingly kisses me back. A bolt of desire shoots through me from the simple act, and I can't resist but to press my tongue past her lips and caress it with hers. Rather than pulling back, tensing, or flinching like I expect her to do, she instead lets out a gasp as she dances her tongue with mine. Our kiss grows in intensity, and a passion I haven't felt since I was a naive young boy who believed in puppy love, causes my cock to harden.

I need to block out all else and focus on Ember. Focus on giving this poor girl a memory that is good. I don't want another first to be stolen from her. I don't know why that is so important to me, but it is. She didn't get the firsts in life, and now that I get to be part of one, I am determined to make it a good one.

And as we kiss, my body awakens, and I want to be inside of her. But I refuse to rush this.

I run my hand over her breasts with the finest touch. I keep my eyes open as I do, watching her face for any sign of distress. But instead, I see her eyes close, her lips open, and ever so slightly, she arches her back to meet my touch. I then trail my fingertips down her belly, inching my way to the space between her legs. I want to see how far I can go before she panics and asks me to stop.

She never does.

Her body's hungry. Needy for touch and affection.

I look at the dress and have no idea how to go about removing it. The buttons are on the back.

"Can you help me get you out of this dress?" I lean down and kiss her softly one more time to try to calm any nerves in her body with the idea of getting naked in front of me. "I'll take my clothes off too."

I need to remove all the barriers because I know she doesn't have the experience or confidence to do it herself or even aid me. She watches me with wide eyes as I lift my shirt over my head revealing my bare chest and abs.

I pause before I move to my pants. "Are you okay with this?"

She nods with more enthusiasm than I've seen and licks her lips again. I try not to smirk and reveal that her face is easy to read. She'd be an awful poker player.

I unbutton and remove my pants completely and kneel before her on the mattress. Her eyes refuse to look down at my dick, and I consider making her but remember how she believed she was so sinful before for stealing a peek. Instead, I turn her around so that I can begin unbuttoning the line of pearl buttons that run from neck to waist.

"You looked beautiful in this dress," I say as she holds up her hair so I can see each pearl.

"Thank you," she says softly.

When the buttons are undone, I lower the fabric slowly off her shoulders and kiss a trail as I do. I haven't kissed a woman's shoulders as I undress her ever before.

I'm not a gentle man in bed. In fact, I can be downright aggressive and nearly primal. The women don't complain, in fact, they can be just as animalistic as me.

But with Ember, I want to be easy and soft.

I want to treat her like the candle of bright light she is, and make sure I don't put out the flame. The flicker of heat from her skin, connecting with my lips nearly makes me explode with a hunger to claim her as mine.

I don't want anyone else to touch her. I don't want anyone to harm her, or scare her, or abuse her in any way. I want to hold her close like fine china to be handled with the utmost care.

Once all our clothes are shed, I lower her back to the bed and place my body over hers. I don't want to frighten her with too much foreplay and foreign acts that she may not be aware of yet. But I also know she isn't ready for me to just take her.

"I don't want this to hurt," I say as I lower my mouth to her lips and kiss her again. "So, I'm going to get you ready with my fingers. I'm going to touch you in a very intimate way if that's okay?"

Would I ever say these words to a woman I was dating or hooking up with? Hell no. In fact, it would probably kill the mood. But Ember was different. She needed this. She needed the steps and the instructions, or I was going to scare the living shit out of her.

I reposition my body so I can reach between her legs more comfortably. I plan to really take my time allowing her body to wake up to arousal. When my fingers touch her pussy, I'm surprised to find her wet. Her tiny moan gives me the permission I need to start massaging the delicate flesh.

"I'm going to put my finger inside of you," I say as I kiss her neck and slightly nibble.

She doesn't answer but nods as I take notice that her breath is coming out more labored and her body tenses as my fingers stroke and spread her lips wide.

I place my finger at her entrance and ease my way in, knowing this is the first thing that has ever been inside of her. Her hips lift and her breath hitches. She places her hands on my back but doesn't stop me. I push my finger deeper inside and her breath turns to a moan.

"Does that feel good?" I ask.

She closes her eyes, bites her lower lip, and nods.

I pull out my finger only to push it back in— a little deeper this time.

"It feels so... it feels so full," she says.

And that is going to be the problem. My dick is far from small, and if my finger is snug in her tight little hole, then this is going to hurt, and I don't want that. Determined to try my best in getting her body accustomed to the stretch, I begin adding the tip of a second finger to open her hole just a little wider. Luckily her juices flow freely, and I have no friction or need for additional lubrication. Her body responds to my touch which has my own body lighting up with fire.

What had started as feeling like I had no choice but to fuck her, has turned into me not being able to picture anything but. I want her. I want Ember possibly more than I have ever wanted anyone before.

"I'm adding a second finger. I need to get you prepared for my size. If this hurts, tell me."

When I add the second finger fully and begin pumping it in and out, Ember opens her eyes and looks at me. "I like it. Is that bad?"

I lean down and kiss her softly on the lips, fingers still inside of her. "That's very good. I want you to like this. I want you to love this."

"Can we do it now?" she asks softly. "I'm ready."

I pull my fingers out and position myself on top of her, nudging her legs further apart with my knees. I make eye contact with her as I position my cock at her entrance. "Are you sure?"

She nods and holds on to my back as I slowly press inside. Once I get the tip in, I pause so she can adjust to the feeling.

"Take me," she says as she pulls me closer to her with her hands and lifts her hips up to force me deeper inside.

With one fluid motion, I press on, feeling the pop of a barrier as she cries out. I pause and kiss her as passionately as I possibly can to distract her from any pain. She kisses me back with just as much desire, and I know I can continue on.

I pull out slowly and then push back in, not feeling the resistance like before. Over and over, I thrust, kissing her as I do. When I pull away just enough to look into her face, I see tears in the corners of her eyes.

"Are you doing okay?" I ask.

"I've never felt so... so close to anyone." A tear falls from her eye as she lifts her head and presses it into my neck.

She holds me tight as we make love for the first time. And though I am taking great care in preventing any discomfort, I still worry. I want her to enjoy this. I want her to look back at this moment and feel nothing but love and tenderness.

"I feel alive," she murmurs against my neck. "I feel free."

In and out, I move, feeling my own level of connection that I struggle to process. This woman in my arms needs me. This woman wants me. This woman is truly giving herself to me. She isn't holding back, or protecting her heart, or thinking of anything else but me. I can feel it. I can feel how wholeheartedly she is giving herself to me.

I feel it.

"Christopher," she moans.

"It's okay, Ember. Allow those feelings to rush in. Don't be afraid."

Her moans deepen and her breath speeds up. Her fingers dig into my back as her body spasms beneath me.

"Come for me," I say as I push my cock deeper inside of her. "Release it all."

Her inner walls milk my cock, and I know I don't have long at all. As she releases a delicate mewl, her head falls back on the mattress, and her eyes are closed in completion.

Not being able to hold back any longer, I pull out of her quickly as a rush of come leaves my body and splatters on her belly. As my body spasms every last bit of completion, I look down on her face and see true bliss. She appears almost spiritual in the way her smile lights up her face.

Very slowly, her eyes open up and she stares up at me with the most perfect blue I have ever seen.

"Thank you," she says. "Thank you."

18

EMBER

I AM FAILING MY HUSBAND.

I know I am, and I don't know what to do about it. I try to cook the best meals I can, although Christopher has to stand by my side and watch as I do since the chain gives us no space. He offers to chop or stir, but I feel as if it's my wifely duty to do it all.

I try to clean our schoolhouse floors and dust all the Nevada desert away, but again, Christopher is right there and feels he needs to help too, or is convincing me I'm being silly trying to clean a prison cell.

I try to make him happy. But he isn't. And each day that passes, I see the dark circles under his eyes intensify and the hollow of his cheeks seem to sink deeper and deeper each hour of our time together.

The man is fading away.

Hallelujah Junction is killing him.

"It's snowing outside," I say as I look out the window. Christopher is simply staring off into space, and I'm desperate to snap him out of the funk he's in.

"Great," he mumbles.

"Papa Rich closed the town to tourists. Which means he may let us out of the schoolhouse soon. We can explore the outside."

Papa Rich had left the two of us alone in the schoolhouse for the most part. He occasionally would enter the room, look around, and then leave as quickly as he came. He didn't seem to taunt Christopher like he did before. If anything, he seemed to be giving us our space so we could get to know each other better.

Christopher leans against his arms on the mattress and stares out the window. "So, now we're really trapped. No people coming. No chance of hope."

Winter also means less visits by Scarecrow which gives me another reason to love this season, so I won't let Christopher bring me down.

"I have something to show you," I say, wondering why I haven't thought of it sooner. It would have helped with Christopher's sour disposition. How could it not?

I move to get off the bed, and Christopher

groans as he joins me. I make my way to a storage closet and pull out an old record player that was left behind from a previous ranger before Papa took over the town. Next to the record player are my prized possessions. Records that fill my heart with love and joy, and in my darkest times can always make me smile.

"Sunshine on my shoulders makes me happy," I say as I set up the player and put a John Denver record on it.

Christopher watches what I'm doing with curiosity. It's the first time today he shows any emotion at all, and though it's not a smile, I'll take it. I'm at least shaking the numbness out of him.

I put the needle on the record where I know my favorite song will start.

I begin humming along and then sing out, "If I had a day that I could give you, I'd give to you a day just like today." I begin swaying back and forth with my eyes closed and just listen. Just feel.

And then I feel Christopher's arms around me. He takes my hands in his and begins to slowly dance with me to the music. I had always dreamed of a day I would dance with a man in a grand ballroom somewhere, but this... this right here, dancing with Christopher, is far better than anything I could dream of.

He kisses the side of my head as he pulls me against his chest. Step by step we dance. His heart beats next to mine. His breath blends with mine. And for the first time since our wedding night, I feel close. I feel Christopher. I haven't lost him to the shadows. Not yet.

"You said you would lend me your happiness," he says against my hair. "I feel I need that right now. I feel myself slipping into a deep, dark hole."

"I'd give you anything," I say, my heart breaking for how sad he is.

"I'm not like you," he says. "I can't shake off the cold chill in my bones like you. I can't see the silver lining. I just see four walls closing in on me."

"I've had practice," I admit. "I know how to fight the demons."

"Well, you're going to have to teach me how."

We keep dancing through song after song on the record player as the snow blankets the ground outside. Our wood-burning stove keeps us warm, but it could be a blizzard inside, and I'd still be warm in Christopher's arms.

I put my hand on his face and giggle. "You have a beard now."

He chuckles. "If my mother could see me now, she'd die of a stroke." His smile quickly fades, and sorrow takes over again.

"I can shave it for you," I offer. "I can borrow a razor from Papa Rich."

"I'll keep the beard," he snaps. He stops dancing and pulls away.

I know me mentioning Papa Rich by name causes Christopher to always lose his temper. I should try to do better and avoid his name at all cost.

I leave the music playing but follow Christopher back to the mattress where we sit.

"I want to make you happy," I say, feeling defeated.

He shifts on the mattress so he can see me directly. "You're a good woman, Ember. You are by far the kindest, most genuine person I've ever met. You don't make me unhappy. It's not you."

"You want to leave."

"I want to leave this place. Yes."

"What about me?" I ask, not sure I want to hear the answer. "What do you feel about me?"

He takes me by the hand. "Confusion, to be honest. A part of me tells me I shouldn't have any feelings for you considering I'm here against my will and chained to you. Another part of me feels this almost neanderthal feeling to protect you and make you mine forever. And whenever I start to allow feelings to form for you, I feel like something's wrong with me. Like I'm sick in the head."

"But aren't I yours forever?" I ask. "We made vows. We're married."

"Ember..." I see pity on his face. "We were forced to marry. You know that right? We were married by a crazy one-legged man. Our marriage isn't even legal. It's not real beyond this town."

"It's real to me!" The words come out much harsher than I want, but I can't help it. And for the first time since being chained to Christopher, I really feel trapped. I snap my hand out of his and cross them protectively against my chest. I want to leave. I want to walk through the tunnel and go to the kitchen so I can get some fresh air that is not also breathed by Christopher, but I can't. "I know we come from different places," I say much calmer. "But vows mean something to me." In a tiny voice as I look at my feet, I add, "You mean something to me."

He reaches for my hand again. I don't want him touching me, but I don't really have a choice. I can't run. I can't even cross the room to be alone.

"I didn't mean to upset you," he says. I look into his eyes and see sincerity. "I can't explain all the feelings I have. I feel weak. I've never felt so weak and out of control in my life. I don't want to give up on my plan for escape, and yet... as each day goes by, I find myself doing exactly that." With his free hand, he moves a piece of my hair behind my ear. "You mean something to me too, Ember. I didn't mean to make you feel otherwise. You mean a lot to me. In fact, I don't think I could have gotten by each day here without you. Your sunshine is the only light in my world right now. I need you."

"I need you."

He leans forward and kisses me softly. His hands cup the sides of my face as if he's afraid I'll pull away.

"I want to please you," I say against the kiss. "I want to please you in all ways."

I lower my hand to the button of his pants and boldly unfasten. I wait for him to stop me or tell me I'm doing it wrong, but he only deepens the kiss. When the pants are loose, I lower my hand and touch his hardness. I take hold of it and feel the weight against my palm. I'd never been so daring before nor sinful—but is it a sin if he's my husband?

I fight against the awkwardness of his clothing and the restriction. As if reading my mind, he lifts up enough so that I can lower everything down, freeing his sex. I glance down, but then feel my face heat.

"This isn't wrong," he rasps out.

I know he's right, and I fight the feelings of sin threatening to suffocate me. Instead, I lower my mouth and kiss the tip of his penis. Unsure, I look up at him. "Is this all right?"

He closes his eyes and leans back. "More than all right."

Feeling a sense of accomplishment that I have brought a smile to his face. I kiss a trail from the head all the way to the base and then lick my way up. The salty musk sends a shiver down my spine. My own sex pulsates in need for him to enter me. I want him again. I want to feel that level of closeness and connection again.

On exhale, he says, "Put me in your mouth. Suck me up and down."

His command forms moisture between my legs, but I do exactly as he asks. Opening my mouth wide, I crawl up on my knees to get a better angle so that I can take all of him.

His hand grips my hair, and he guides my head down and then tugs me back up. We repeat this action several times with his moans growing in intensity with each time. I drag my tongue along his flesh and love the power that I have. I'm giving him pleasure and I know it. I love it. I love the control.

I realize I can tighten my lips and he groans. I can go deeper into the back of my throat and his hips buck. His actions are the result of mine. I'm finally feeling like a wife who can please my husband.

"Ember," I hear Papa Rich call from the tunnel.

He doesn't usually give warning, but thank goodness he is. I jump up and when I see that Christopher isn't moving in the slightest to pull his pants back on, I panic. He's going to push Papa's buttons. I can see it in his eyes.

"Please," I beg, tugging his pants up the best I can.

Christopher sighs, rolls his eyes, but pulls up his pants right as Papa Rich enters from the tunnel.

He stops and looks at me, then Christopher with that suspicious eye I know of his. "Christopher, it's nice to see you look as if you're getting comfortable in your new home."

Christopher smirks and remains leaned back on the mattress. "Very."

Papa Rich looks at me and I know my face must be several shades of red. "And are the two of you getting along good?"

"Extremely," Christopher says with a twinkle in his eye.

I see Papa's jaw tighten and his eyes narrow.

I hold my breath. I don't want Papa to think we're sinners and feel we have to pay penance for our actions. Christopher doesn't seem concerned at all. His hardness is still very visible beneath his pants, and I wonder if tossing a blanket over him will be too obvious.

"I'm running into town," he says to me as he clears his throat. "I saw your usual grocery list on the fridge. Is there anything else you need?"

"Yes, actually." I say softly. "Is it possible to pick up a razor for Christopher? In case he wants to shave his beard."

I figure that Christopher should have the option,

and I know that him borrowing anything from Papa was out of the question and even angered him. At least this way, he will have something of his own.

Papa Rich nods. "Anything else?" He actually looks at Christopher and waits for him to answer.

"Yeah. How about a bottle of Jack?" Christopher says with a cocky grin.

Papa surprises me when he says, "I don't see why not. I'll add it to the list."

I see the cocky look on Christopher's face disappear and something unfamiliar takes its place. He's angry. He knows Papa is playing his game right back. Two men who have fury bubbling up inside but neither will show it.

"Sugar," I add, hating the tension in the room. "I'll make us a cake."

Papa nods again and then goes back into the tunnel.

"You drink?" I ask, knowing Papa Rich rarely did.

He shrugs. "I used to drink a lot. Maybe too much." He chuckles. "This place has been the worst detox known to man."

"Why?" I ask. "Why too much?"

"Life," he says almost sadly. "In some crazy way, being here made me realize that I was in some sort of prison of my own in New York. I think I was self-medicating."

"Booze is a medicine?" I know I'm sheltered from all the things in the outside world, but I have never heard of alcohol being medicinal.

"Just a saying. But it did seem to make me function better. Pills and whisky were my go to." He looks at me. "Like I said though, this place broke me of that habit cold turkey."

"Do you miss it?"

"No." Christopher hops off the bed and walks to the window, jerking me alongside him. "How often does he go to town in the winter?"

"Not as often," I say.

"How long is he gone when he does?"

I shrug. "I'm not sure. A couple of hours with good weather, but the snow slows him down."

Christopher's face lights up and he looks at me. "He's gone for hours?"

I nod. I know what he's thinking. What he's hoping.

He's wrong.

There's no way out of here.

There's no way.

"Is there any other vehicle here? Another ranger truck? Anything?"

I shake my head.

Christopher stares out the window waiting for Papa Rich to leave. The glass fogs up with our breaths, and he wipes at the glass for a better view.

"What about the ranger's office? A phone? There has to be a phone."

"Papa has a radio, and he takes it with him. I told you this. No phone. No way out."

"How do you know there's no phone? How do you know? We need to go see for ourselves."

I reach for his hand to try to soothe his wild mind. "I know, Christopher. There's no phone, he locks everything, and he's thought of every possibility. Trust me. I know."

I hate that I'm stealing his hope. I can't stand that I'm the reason his face is falling from excited to despair.

I so desperately want to be the good wife.

I want to please. I want to please more than anything.

"We can look if you want."

Although I already know it will be useless, he needs to see for himself. He needs to walk down the path of hopelessness on his own. I can only hold his hand and be by his side as he does so... as a dutiful wife.

19

CHRISTOPHER

I REFUSE TO GIVE UP HOPE. DAY AFTER DAY AND I refuse. The snow is thick, the air heavy with evil, and all I can do is sit and wait. There will be a time. There will be an opening of opportunity, and I will take it.

I have to hand it to Richard.

The man is smart.

There is no phone, no way to reach the outside world. Ember is right about that.

I have no idea where he hides his keys to the truck even though I look around the kitchen every time we are there to prepare meals. I know I will have one shot, and I don't want to be reckless or foolish when I make the move. I have to be patient. The time will come. I know it will.

"We should start prep for supper soon. I want

to make a special recipe of mine for you," Ember says as we sit near the wood stove.

I give her a smile because I know how hard she tries to keep me happy. I wish she could meet the real me. I wish she could see the man I truly am when I'm not shackled and captured against my will. I think she'd like me better. I think she'd feel more loved because I would have more to offer. I would have a soul that wasn't shattered into a million pieces. I am barely hanging on in here. I feel as if the monster of this place is eating me alive, and though I try hard not to take it out on Ember, I know I do. I see the pain in her eyes when I snap. I see her desperate need to fill my days with the rainbows and flowers she imagines, but I just can't. I know she wants me to be the Prince Charming she had always fantasized. I know I should be better.

I just can't.

Not while being here.

Not here in Hallelujah Junction. But if we ever leave... if we ever leave, I'll be a better man.

Movement outside the window catches my eye. I'd seen deer, rabbit and squirrels before, but something in my gut tells me this time is different. This time I need to pay attention.

"Come to the window," I say, not wanting to just drag Ember with me to get a better look.

We make our way to the window, and my heart stops.

Two people snowshoeing in the town below.

"They aren't supposed to be here," Ember whispers. I hear the fear in her voice, but I can't help but feel a sense of excitement that nearly paralyzes me.

My instinct is to bang on the window and start screaming, but I also don't know where Richard is. I don't want to reveal our guests by making a commotion.

"We need to go outside," I say, spinning around and nearly causing Ember to fall because she's not ready.

She reaches for my hand. "Christopher, we can't."

I glare at her so she knows I mean business. I don't want to be mean to her, but I will if I have to. "This is our chance. I'm not going to stand here and miss it."

"If Papa Rich sees us leave the schoolhouse, he may lock us in the cellar and never allow us to come back here again. We'll lose his trust." She looks around the small structure that had become our home with tears in her eyes. "We were just getting comfortable."

"Now, Ember. Now." No patience or understanding is left in my body. "Now."

I take a step forward with my chained leg, and if I have to drag her along, I will.

She walks beside me, but I can sense her internal struggle.

"Pine Cone. Where's my cat? I can't leave her."

"We'll come back for her. I promise," I say, not wanting to waste time hunting down her cat.

"Please don't make me do this," she begs softly. "He'll find us. He will."

"We just need to get to them before he does."

"He knows they're here. I'm telling you, Christopher, he knows." There's urgency in her voice, but I don't care. This is our shot. It could be our only one.

I open the door to the schoolhouse, and even that defiant act has Ember gasping.

"We're barefoot," she states. "We can't just walk out there in the snow."

"We can, and we will."

If I have to, I am willing to lose both my feet to frostbite if it means escaping. I hope I don't have to, and I most certainly don't want that for Ember, but if the sacrifice has to be made, then so be it.

There isn't a lot of slack in the chain connecting us, but I believe I can pick Ember up if need be. It will be awkward but can still be done. But not yet. We need to reach the couple before they get too far away. I need Ember to run at the same pace as me.

"Just focus on running and keeping your foot at

the same speed as me. We'll worry about the cold effects later."

We don't have time to plan, and we don't have time to discuss this further, so I jerk her out of the schoolhouse and begin running as fast as Ember's footing can go.

The couple comes into sight and I consider screaming at the top of my lungs. But they are still far enough away that for them to hear me, means that I have to be loud enough for Richard to also hear me. So, instead, I begin waving my arms frantically in hopes they see us coming.

"A little faster," I say as I wrap my arm around Ember to keep her close at my side and to prevent her from stumbling.

"It's too cold," she says. "We're going to lose our toes. We should go back before it's too late."

I ignore her complaints just as I ignore any discomfort in my feet. Escape is so close.

So close.

We are getting close enough now that I can actually see their expressions on their faces. They're happy, they're excited to be spending their day playing in the snow. They have no idea what they are about to see. They are both in their twenties and give off the puppy love vibe. So innocent. So free from worry. So in love without a care in the world.

Then the boy sees me. His expression turns from joy to confusion.

The girl sees me next, and her smile morphs to a look of fear. She sees the chain around our ankles and backs behind her partner for protection.

"Help us," I call out as we approach. "Help."

The male fully steps in front of the female as a shield, and though we are the ones asking for help, I can imagine what kind of sight we must be.

"You have to get us out of here," I say, still hobbling up to them with Ember at my side. "There's a crazy man here who's kidnapped us. Call 911 now, but we need to get to your car. Now."

"What the fuck?" the man says as he looks down and sees that Ember and I are both barefoot, nearly ankle deep in the snow that we keep sinking into with every step.

"Oh my God," the woman says as her body visibly trembles. "You were kidnapped?"

"We don't have time to talk. Where's your car?"

The woman is pulling out her phone with wide eyes. She looks down at the screen and frowns. "There's no signal."

"We need to get out of here now," I say, while the man nods in agreement.

He points to our right. "We're down the hill some. The snow made it too hard for us to drive to the parking lot. We're going to have to hike a bit to our Jeep." He looks back at our feet. "You can't make it barefoot."

"Here," the woman says, as she takes off her gloves. "Try to put these on your feet."

She hands her gloves to Ember and bends down to help cover her feet. The man does the same with his gloves and gives them to me. Anything is better than nothing, and I'm grateful for the idea and the offer.

The woman then takes off her coat and gives it to Ember. "Don't worry," she says. "I have warm winter clothes on underneath."

The man follows her and does the same, giving me his coat. "Come on," he says. "Let's get you both out of here."

I see Ember look around with panic in her eyes. She's searching for Richard, and I just pray we get out of here fast enough.

"Hurry," I say as the four of us start running in the direction of the Jeep.

The gloves make it difficult to run, but the chain around Ember's and my ankle make it near impossible. I decide to try to pick her up which causes the cuff around my ankle to dig into my flesh, but I ignore the pain. She clings to my shoulders to try to hold on as I plow through the snow with a mission to survive. I can nearly feel the breath of Richard behind me.

He's coming.

I know he's coming.

We just have to get out of the town and down the hill to the Jeep before he reaches us.

Run.

Run.

Run faster.

The couple are running in their snowshoes which allows them to be ahead of me, but they both keep turning and looking over their shoulders to make sure we're close behind. The snowshoes carve a path for me which helps. I'm not sinking down nearly as much in the packed-down snow they create.

"We're almost there," the male says.

I'm afraid to look over my shoulder. I'm worried that if I do, I'll see Richard charging forward with evil and vengeance in his eyes. He'll kill me if he catches us. I have no doubt he will. He'll kill me and he'll torture Ember. He'll also kill this innocent couple who are only trying to help us.

Run.

Run.

Ignore the cold.

Run.

Even if Richard doesn't see us yet, it won't be hard to track us. I can see blood coming from both my and Ember's ankle. The metal cuff has nearly rubbed us both raw and down to the bone. Our path of blood we leave behind is our own personal bread crumb left for the witch who will boil our bodies alive if found.

Ember is silent.

She hasn't said much since we left the schoolhouse. I want to soothe her. I want to comfort her in some way. I want to tell her everything will be all right, but I don't want to lie. I have no idea if this escape attempt will be successful, and until we're in the back seat of the Jeep heading down the road, I won't issue a single word of reassurance. I know she's scared... but I can only focus on marching through the snow one step at a time.

And then I see the Jeep.

Oh Jesus Christ, I see the Jeep.

Freedom is on the horizon and we are nearly there.

My heart skips, my blood boils with renewed energy and determination to pick up my speed. Safety. We are so close to safety.

We're going to get the hell out of Hallelujah Junction!

"That's it," the man says as he and the woman keep shoeing ahead. "Hurry up. We're almost there."

The male opens the back door to the Jeep and helps me and Ember into the back seat while the woman crawls into the front seat. The man then runs around to the driver's side of the Jeep.

I remove the soaked gloves from my feet which somehow had stayed on and begin massaging feeling back into my feet. Ember is frozen in place and doesn't move.

"Try to get your feet warmed up," I say, but notice she doesn't budge.

"He's going to find us," she says softly which has the girl turn her head to look at her in fear.

"Who?" the girl asks. "Who is going to find us? Who kidnapped you?" She reaches for her phone again, but when she puts it back down, I know she still has no signal.

"We're safe now," I say, taking hold of Ember's foot and removing the glove.

Her foot looks red from the snow, but doesn't look like any frostbite is present, which is the same for my feet.

And just as hope begins to warm my frozen body, the sound of the Jeep *not* turning over happens. The Jeep won't start.

"Come on!" the man says as he keeps trying but nothing.

"Why won't it start?" the woman beside him screeches in terror.

I glance toward the road and know there is no way that Ember and I can make it down the road wearing nothing but gloves on our feet. The couple maybe can...

"You both need to get out of here, now," I say,

feeling like I can hear the sound of boots crunching on the snow. "He'll kill you. You need to run."

"We can't just leave you," the man says as he keeps trying to start the Jeep.

"Get down the hill and call the police," I order, scanning the area for any signs of Richard.

The woman hops out of the Jeep and turns and looks at us. "I promise we'll come back for you."

Ember doesn't say anything but removes the woman's coat and hands it to me. I remove the coat given to me and hand both of them to the woman.

"Run as fast as you can. This man, Richard, is insane. He's extremely dangerous."

The couple doesn't waste any time and start snowshoeing down the hill. Ember and I crawl out of the back seat and hobble our way to the driver's side of the Jeep. I jump into the seat and try to start the vehicle myself. It's making no sound at all. It's not even trying. I get out of the Jeep and open the hood of the engine. I'm no mechanic, but maybe Lady Luck will shine down on me, and I'll see something that's an easy fix.

"We need to go back to the schoolhouse," Ember says. "Maybe if we get back there before Papa Rich notices we're missing, then this will be like nothing happened."

I stop staring at all the guts of the Jeep and look at her in the eyes. She has a point. If the couple makes it down the hill and is able to reach the authorities, then it's just a matter of time until we're rescued. But if we show our hand, and we have Richard chasing after them... Maybe trying to get back to the schoolhouse undetected is a good idea.

"Okay," I say, nodding. "Let's get back."

I never thought I'd be going *back* to the schoolhouse if I ever got my chance of escape, and yet, here I am.

We quickly run back to Hallelujah Junction, scanning the area for any signs of Richard. Excuses were running through my head as to what we will tell him if he catches us outside. I decide to remove the gloves from both of our feet and bury them in some snow just in case we are detected. Maybe I can convince him that Ember and I were going stir crazy and had to get out... barefoot or not. I know it's a stretch, but I have to tell the man something. Ember, however, doesn't have a lying bone in her body. The chances of her getting away with a lie is about as impossible as escaping this godforsaken town.

"If your father notices the tracks in the snow," I say as we get closer and closer to the school, "tell him we wanted to play in the snow."

"He'll know the truth," she says. "He always knows everything."

"Ember," I snap. "You need to listen to me. Tell him we went for a quick walk. Nothing else."

A new fear forms. Ember.

If she tells Richard about the couple, he may try to hide us or even relocate. He may go on the run and take us with him to avoid authorities. Hell... he may kill us both to hide any evidence of kidnapping.

"We went for a walk to get some fresh air," I reiterate. "Are we clear?"

She nods, but I don't really believe her. And as we open the door to the schoolhouse—our prison —I just pray to a God I don't know that I believe in any longer that the couple is reaching civilization and getting help quick.

I SEE OUR PRINTS ALL OVER THE TOWN BELOW. IF I can see them, then I know Papa Rich can too. There are so many, and two sets have snowshoes. There is no way to explain this. There is no way out.

"Shit," Christopher sees what I do outside the schoolhouse window. "We need to somehow hide all those."

It's snowing but not hard enough. Not fast enough.

Mother Nature is not on our side.

We both have our feet wrapped in a blanket from our bedding, warming them up. I can't imagine going back into the snow now.

"I don't see how we can," I say.

"Okay…" Christopher begins. "We tell him that

you and I went for a quick walk outside to enjoy the fresh air. When we were down there, we saw the snowshoe tracks, but saw nothing else. We need to keep to this story."

I nod for Christopher's sake, but I already know we are doomed. Papa Rich knows. I know he knows.

"We just have to buy enough time for them to reach the authorities," he says. He turns to look at me with a look of determination in his eyes. "If he finds out, or if he tries to move all of us, we have to fight him. Do you hear me? We have to do whatever we can to fight the man."

I shake my head as tears well in my eyes.

"Ember, I need you to be strong. I need you to listen to me."

"Christopher—"

"I'm your husband!" he shouts. When I flinch, he softens his facial expression. "I'm sorry for yelling. But I'm your husband and you need to trust me. You need to have faith that I'm going to get us out of this. You just have to be on my team. *My* team."

"I'm scared," I admit.

"I know. But we're so close. We just need time."

Father Time is not on our side either.

Because the next voice I hear is Papa Rich's. "Trust," he begins as he slams the door to the tunnel. "Trust is something that should never be abused."

He knows.

He knows.

Christopher turns to face him without the slightest show of fear. "Let me guess," he begins as he crosses his arms against his chest. "You're annoyed that Ember and I went for a walk? Are we expected to never go outside and see the snow? Ember said that when the tourists leave, we can move about the town more freely."

"Very true," Papa Rich says calmly.

"So then why are you standing there as if we did something wrong?" Christopher asks.

I stare down at my feet when Papa Rich looks into my eyes. I can't face him. I can't lie, and he knows it.

"I know you think that you are the head of the household now that you are married to Ember. That you make the rules," he begins. "But not in Hallelujah Junction. I make the rules here. I oversee this kingdom."

Christopher sighs. "Note taken. We'll remain inside. Anything else?"

"Ember?" Papa Rich says, forcing me to look up at him. "We talk about consequences all the time. You know all about them."

I nod. "Yes, sir. But like Christopher said, we

just went for a walk. It was quick because of the snow on our feet."

I had never lied to my father before, and it surprises me how easily the words flow from my mouth.

An evil grin forms on his face as he pulls out his pistol and points it at Christopher.

"Papa!" I scream. "No! Don't kill him. Please!"

Christopher calmly puts up his arms in surrender and says, "Richard, you need to think this through. You don't want my murder on your hands. Who will take care of Ember when you go to jail? You think she can survive out in that world without you *and* me? Think of Ember right now." He glances out the window and then back at the gun. "You know the police are coming. You know this. So, think about the bigger picture. Think about what happens if you kill me. What happens to your daughter?"

"Both of you walk," he demands as he points toward the front door of the schoolhouse. "Don't try anything stupid, son," he warns. "I'll shoot your dick off before I kill you. I won't make your death quick. Listen to every command I say or else."

"Papa, you have this all wrong," I try to lie again, but I walk beside Christopher toward the door as I do.

"Out," Papa demands as we exit into the snow.

"To the mill," he says, stabbing the gun into Christopher's back.

The mill?

No!

He's going to push Christopher into the pits! That's the consequence. That's what we get for trying to escape. Even if the couple reaches the police, it will be too late. Christopher will be burned alive by the acid. He'll be dead! No!

The chain rattling between our ankles remind me that there is no chance of running. The gun stabbing Christopher's back as we shuffle our way through the snow brings me to a reality I can't face. There's no hope. No hope. I also know that once Papa Rich has his mind set on something, there is no convincing him otherwise.

Christopher has failed him.

Consequences must be given.

Blood must be shed.

The Devil must be conquered.

No!

I reach out and hold Christopher's hand. My last connection. My last touch of the man I have grown to love. He doesn't deserve this and yet... he will pay for his act. I know there is no way out. No way will Papa allow this crime to go unpunished.

"Papa," I begin, but then stop speaking as we enter the mill. I know my breath is wasted. I've been here before. I know what happens.

"In the garden of evil, someone must pay," Papa says as he leads us to the dangerous acid pit that sits in the middle of the mill.

We walk past the warning signs and even yellow caution tape. We maneuver around the broken planks that hang all around us. It's Hell we have entered.

It's dark.

It's cold.

And as we approach the pit closer, I see what the Devil has waiting for us.

"You son of a bitch," Christopher says, as he sees what I do. "You're sick. You're evil."

"I'm merely the messenger of God. Someone must pay for our sins," Papa Rich says.

On the other side of the pit is the couple we met tied at the ankles and wrists. They are also tied to a wooden beam, helpless and afraid. Their mouths are gagged though I don't see the point in that. No one is around who can hear their screams. When they see us, they both try to struggle against their binds with absolute terror in their eyes. It's almost as if they hope we can save them.

We can't save you.

"Trespassers must be punished," Papa Rich begins like he has in the past when he's about to push guilty tourists to their death.

"No!" Christopher shouts. "Let them go! They did nothing."

Papa Rich gives a slanted grin. "Did you think you would get away with it? Did you think I didn't know they were here? Did you think I'd allow for you to steal my daughter and drive away in that Jeep?" He shakes his head. "No. Amazing how fast you can disable a vehicle with a few pulls of some cables. And shocking how trusting the two were when I pulled up beside them in my ranger's truck. They thought I was there to help." He laughs. "You all underestimated your opponent, and now must pay the price."

He reaches down to a bunch of bags by his feet with the gun still pointing at Christopher. Pulling out rope, he begins to wrap it around our ankle chain and then ties us to another beam directly across from the couple.

"Put out your wrists," Papa demands.

Christopher, who appears stunned as his eyes remain pinned on the innocent couple across the way, puts out his wrists. I do the same and Papa ties us both with the rope. It's tight and rubs our skin raw almost immediately.

Now we are as trapped as they are.

"First, we punish you," he says to Christopher. He pulls out a switchblade and opens it to reveal the blade.

"When you weep upon their graves, you may someday be forgiven, but first you must pay your penance."

Papa shoves us both to the ground where we are sitting among the ancient wooden boards. He takes hold of Christopher's foot and slashes the bottom of it with the knife.

Christopher closes his eyes and hisses out in pain, but does nothing more to fight it.

Papa slices again, and again. Striping the bottom of Christopher's foot with one bloody cut after another.

"Thou shall not run again," Papa Rich says as he reaches for Christopher's other foot and begins slicing the flesh on that one as well.

Blood trickles down Papa's wrist as he holds Christopher's foot up, carving his penance into his body.

I see the pain on Christopher's face, but he never cries out. He remains stoic in his punishment. And though I want to scream out and beg Papa to stop, I also feel a sense of hope. If this is Christopher's only punishment, then maybe he will be spared from the pits. Maybe he won't be sacrificed for our sins. Maybe Papa will have mercy. Maybe Christopher will have to bleed but not stop breathing.

Finally, Papa stops, puts away his bloody switchblade and stands. His dark eyes stare me down. "You've been bad, Ember. So very bad. And what happens next is your punishment. It will be your worst discipline yet."

Now that we are unable to run or attack Papa, he tucks the gun into his belt and walks toward the couple. I watch him as he is careful where he steps because one wrong or careless move and it will be Papa Rich in the acid pit instead of them. I used to hold my breath in the past, fearful that Papa Rich would fall, and I would lose him forever. But now…

Now I watch him in hopes that he will slip.

He needs to join the Devil. His time has come.

God help me, I know his time has come.

"Have no fear," he says to the couple as he nears. "Either God will guide you to the gates of Heaven, or the Devil will be there to pull you into the depths of Hell. I am not the one to judge. Your maker will do that. Pray that you have done enough good in this world to help make His decision easy."

Both begin squirming against the ropes and screaming behind the gags. No one faces death with bravery. Everybody I've watched fall into the pits have fought and screamed until the very end.

Papa Rich turns and points his finger at Christopher and me. "You both did this. Their deaths are on you. Your hands drip with their blood. May God forgive you."

"He's really going to do this," I hear Christopher say under his breath. "A madman."

I can only imagine the thoughts and horror going through Christopher's mind. I still remember the first time I watched someone fall to their death. And though it never gets easier, the one thing that has changed for me is that I know there is nothing I can do to stop it. I've begged in the past, swore to do anything I could. I thought I could recite the Bible or try to reach Papa's heart somehow in the past.

Nothing.

This will happen no matter what we say or do.

Papa pulls out his gun again in case the man or woman get any ideas to try to fight him off as he unfastens the rope. They should fight. They should take the bullet over what will come next. They should choose a fast death over the pits any day, but none of them do. They all comply in some foolish hope that Papa Rich won't follow through if they just be good. If they do as he asks, he will save them.

They are all wrong.

As the couple stand side by side, Papa Rich removes their gags. He always removes the gags because he likes to hear them beg. He likes to hear them scream as their flesh sizzles from their bones.

"Please," the man says first. "We'll leave here and pretend we never came."

"Don't do this," the woman says between sobs. "Please. We won't say a thing. Just let us go."

"Richard!" Christopher shouts. "Let them go and punish me. This is all on me. They did nothing wrong but be in the wrong place at the wrong time. Take me."

"They trespassed. There are signs. They are the rule breakers and must be punished."

Not waiting another moment, Papa Rich shoves the girl and then the man with enough force to make them fall over the edge into the pit of water. Oily, black, mineral-based, and full of acid that no one can survive.

Both scream on the way down, followed by a splash. Then an ear-piercing howl as their bodies struggle to climb the walls as the liquid eats at their skin.

Christopher leans forward which also forces me to. I know he wants to see for himself, although his soul is screaming for him to close his eyes and block it all out. But it's impossible. I've tried. Oh how I've tried.

Looking the other way only makes you see it over and over in your nightmares instead. You must face the horror head on as your blood turns cold and your inner self melts along with the poor souls dying below.

The screams rattle the rafters above and dust falls down upon us.

Their sounds of agony will forever be with me. I will forever be the keeper of their charred and stolen spirits. They are locked inside of me with all the others.

Papa Rich stands and watches. He's proud. He's done what he considers his Godly duty. He always looks the same.

Dark eyes, firm jaw, and arms at his side. And then when the last gurgled scream happens, he raises his hands to the sky as if in offering to God.

21

CHRISTOPHER

"WHAT HAVE YOU DONE?" I HISS AS I STRUGGLE TO hold on to sanity.

Richard walks toward us slowly. "It's what *you've* done, son. You did this. Those poor people are dead because of you."

My eyes dart to Ember who has tears running down her face, but she seems to have a look of acceptance. There is no outrage, or even fear. She just sits with her head down and in silent sorrow.

And if I didn't understand her fear and how controlled she is by Richard before, I do now. If she has had to witness this awful... Fuck... if she had to watch this before... I can't even—

It isn't just having to watch two people die in the most horrific way possible that has my mind reeling. It's also the knowledge that any chance of escape is crushed and will forever be. The burning in my feet from the wounds is nothing to the pain in my entire core. Defeat and loss of hope is far worse than a cut of a blade.

"And now, Ember, it is your time to suffer your consequences," Richard says as he walks past us.

I position my body in front of Ember to the best that I can considering the ties. "You leave her the fuck alone."

I'll die before I'll let him touch her. I will follow that couple into the pits before I will let Richard harm her in any way.

He ignores my threat and leaves the mill.

I pull Ember closer. "I won't let him hurt you."

She looks up at me with tears in her eyes. "I'm sorry, Christopher. I'm sorry."

"Don't ever apologize for that man. He's not you. You have no control over that crazy."

"Those poor people…"

"*You* didn't do that. *I* didn't do that," I lean forward and kiss her cheek.

"I knew what would happen. I knew. I should have never let us leave the schoolhouse." She looks at the pit. "Now they're dead." She looks at my bloody feet. "How much pain are you in?"

Before I can answer, Richard reenters the mill holding Ember's cat in his arms.

Ember instantly cries out and starts shaking her head.

"No, Papa. No. Please no!"

"You are to blame for this, Ember," Richard says as he approaches the pits with the cat. "It broke my heart watching you try to run away from our home. Our home! You allowed sin to enter our home! You know better. I raised you better."

"I'm so sorry. I truly am. I'll do anything. Just please let Pine Cone go."

The cat tries to break free from Richard's grasp and meows in distress as she does. He only holds tighter and shakes his head.

"You must be punished."

Without another word, Richard tosses the cat into the pit and the sound of Ember's scream mixed with the hissing and screeching of the cat nearly drives me mad. It's the worst sound I have ever heard in my entire life. Pain of the animal mixed with agony of its owner nearly destroys me.

I hold onto Ember as she lurches toward the pit, ripping her skin with the rope and chain. If it weren't for her confines, I have no doubt Ember would throw herself into the pit in hopes of saving her cat.

"No!" she wails. "No! No! No!"

"Hear your cat suffer, girl. Listen to your beloved pet pay for your crimes. Listen to the suffering it must endure."

Ember collapses against me and cries out in the

most heart-wrenching and devastated way imaginable.

I kiss her head. I hold her close. I hold her ears so she doesn't have to hear the cat struggle.

I try to soothe her as she claws at me in a desperate need to be free. But I refuse to let her hear. I refuse to let her experience this any longer if I can ease it at all.

"Pine Cone!" she cries out. "No, no, no."

And then the room grows silent.

No more victims.

No more deaths.

All that remains are the ghosts of the murdered haunting us all.

Finally, Richard speaks. "I will untie you now. I trust you to find your way back to the schoolhouse. I have to finish cleaning up the mess you both made and hide the Jeep and all signs of the couple."

He moves toward us with pistol in hand in case I choose to do anything. And if it weren't for the gun, I'd plow into his body, driving him into the pit myself, not caring if he pulls me with him.

"I will burn down your entire world. I swear this," I spat at him, not caring about the consequences. How much worse can they be? What I just witnessed was far worse than anything a sane person could imagine.

He nods, pats an inconsolable Ember on the top of the head. "What I did was harsh," he says. "I had to in order to make sure that the two of you don't ever make this foolish mistake again. God expects me to watch over the two of you. My family. Always my family."

The man needs to die at whatever cost.

But for now, as the rope is removed and Richard leaves us, I focus all my attention on the broken woman beside me who hasn't stopped crying. She can barely breathe between her body-wracking sobs.

"Come on, Ember. Let's get back," I say softly as I lift her to standing. Devastation has weakened her, and I worry if she'll be able to walk at all. "It's freezing, and we need to get back to where it's warm."

I somehow get us back to our four-wall prison, though we both walk in a daze. I wonder if Ember will ever stop crying, and I wonder if I will ever feel like a human again.

Did I do this?

Am I to blame for the deaths?

I want to say no. I want to blame Richard, but I'm the one who forced Ember to leave. I brought my crisis to the innocent couple. I made their problems my own. I expected them to help even though it cost them their lives.

She hiccups, chokes on her tears, and then starts the morose melody all over again. She allows me to rub heat back into her feet by the wood burning stove, but doesn't speak, doesn't make eye contact, doesn't acknowledge me at all.

Her blonde hair hangs in her face, covering her red-blotched, tear-soaked face, and I have never wanted to hold someone as much before. I also want to scream and rage against Richard, but I don't know where Ember's breaking point is, and I worry one more harsh word will send her over the cliff of sanity never to return again.

"Pine Cone," Ember moans as she curls up on the mattress after I stoke the fire. "My Pine Cone."

I crawl up behind her and spoon her body next to mine. Wrapping my arms around her, I kiss the back of her head and try to comfort. "I'm so sorry, Ember. So sorry."

"Why would he do this? Why?" Her cries intensify.

"Because he's a bad man. He's crazy." I'm careful not to allow my rage to show through and manage to keep my voice even and calm.

I want her to face the facts, but I know I must be easy and tentative in getting there. The only thing good that could come from this nightmarish incident is that Ember may finally see her father for the psychopath he is. She may not resist me so much in planning our escape. She may even become a willing participant once her nearly paralyzing grief subsides some.

Her body shakes as her sobs fill the empty space of the room.

"I promise you; I'll get us out of here. I promise."

She spins away from me and sits up with outrage in her eyes. "Like last time?" she screams. She points at me accusingly. "You didn't listen! I told you what would happen. I told you that we'd get caught. I warned you!"

Fury blazes in her eyes and her sobs blend with her screams.

I reach out to her calmly. "I'm sorry. If I could take away your pain, I would."

She snaps her arm away and turns so her back is to me. "You didn't believe me when I told you there is no way out. He knows everything. I've watched for years how he works. I know you think I'm weak and scared. You thought that because you are stronger than me you could outsmart him." She spins her face to glare at me. "You were wrong! If you had just listened, those people would still be alive. My cat would still be here with me!"

"Hate me if it takes away your pain," I say. "Blame me. Crucify me in all ways. I'd prefer anything else but to know you hurt."

"I don't hate you," she says softly between sniffles. "I just feel so... lost. I feel like I'm sinking and drowning in a hole of despair. I wish Papa Rich would have just pushed me in the pit. I'm so tired. So tired."

I inch to her and take her into my arms from behind. She tenses but doesn't push me away. "I love you, Ember. I love you and wish I had no part in causing you this misery."

She slowly turns her head to look at me with red-rimmed eyes, wipes at her nose, and asks, "You love me?"

I pull her close. "I do. I love you and will do whatever I can to make sure this never happens to you again."

She begins to cry again, harder. "There's nothing you can do. This is our forever, Christopher. Fake happiness, false hope, and nothing but dark and evil. I lied to you when I told you that you could borrow from my happiness. I never had any. I know only sadness and loneliness. I'm a liar. I'm a liar and God finally punished me today. This is all my fault."

"No, Ember." I stroke her hair and squeeze her to me. "There's one person to blame, and he'll pay someday. He'll pay."

"Face reality, Christopher. Trust me. It's the only way."

Broken.

My captured bride now finally reveals just how shackled she is.

"I'll save us. I will."

I lower her down to the bed and hold her close as she cries herself to sleep.

Closing my eyes, I see the couple.

Haunted. I will forever be haunted.

22

CHRISTOPHER

I WAKE TO EMBER HOLDING MY FOOT AS SHE examines it. She notices I'm awake and says, "We need to get these cuts cleaned up. I'm worried they'll get infected. We shouldn't have gone to sleep with them like this." She furrows her brow and looks at the bed. "We got blood and dirt on our bedding. I'll have to do the wash today."

If it weren't for her puffy and blood-shot eyes, I wouldn't know she had nearly died of a broken heart last night. She almost seems like my normal Ember again.

I sit up and cup her cheek. "I'm not worried about my feet. I'm worried about you."

She gently pulls away from my touch. "I'm fine. I'm not the one with gashes on my feet."

She reminds me of my mother right now. When my father died, my mother gave herself a mere twenty-four hours to mourn and cry, and then it was as if she locked all the emotions inside, never to reveal where the key was. No mention of my father again, all pictures and memories stored away, clothing boxed and donated. She simply wiped him away. Not a single tear was shed again.

Survival.

Ember knows how to survive.

No time for tears in survival.

Knowing that Ember will not be happy until she can tend to my feet, I hobble over to the pitcher of water by the wood stove.

"We'll wash it up first. But I may need to go to the main house to get antiseptic and bandages." She begins to wipe at my feet and focuses on her mission. "Yes, we need to get to the main house. I can't clean these enough with what I have here."

I consider asking her if she's okay but see that she doesn't want to relive yesterday. She's moving forward as if nothing horrific happened, and I need to allow it. I need to allow her to cope with tragedy however she does. Clearly, she is an expert at it.

Instead, I need to focus on what happens next for us.

We need a plan.

I don't think going back to the main house is a good idea. I don't want to face Richard yet, and I don't think Ember should either. The homicidal thoughts in me are strong, and I'm not sure I'd be rational when facing the man so soon after his monstrous acts. But I also know that is where the food is. I'm also half expecting for him to arrive today and force us back into the cellar.

He should.

He should expect that I will only try to escape again with more vengeance.

The only lesson he has taught me is that I need to get out of here now. There is never going to be the right time. He's a smart man who I didn't give enough credit to. I thought I could outwit him, but now... I know I have to just force the hand. I have to *make* the escape happen at whatever cost.

Leaving us in the schoolhouse with only a chain around our ankles will be his biggest mistake. Underestimating our level of fear and that it will control us from this point on, is a crucial mistake. I don't fear the man will kill me. No... my true fear is that I will spend the rest of my life in Hallelujah Junction. And after yesterday... I will die trying to escape rather than spend more time here. He should have pushed me in the acid pits. He will regret that he didn't.

And it's not just about me anymore. Ember is in the mix. I meant it when I told her last night that I loved her. I do. What that means, and what that looks like, I have no idea. Nothing is normal with her and me, but that doesn't take away the emotions I have for her inside. Were they forced upon me? Yes, but regardless how they came, they still exist.

If I can only make one captive vow, it will be to save this woman.

It is no longer about me.

I will save Ember until my last breath.

I prefer to end up in the pit of acid before accepting our life here.

"He'll avoid us today," she says as if reading my mind. "He always avoids me for days after... after consequences."

"He won't be at the main house?" I ask.

She shakes her head. "Maybe he's ashamed." She swallows hard. "He should be."

"Where does he go?"

She shrugs. "Sometimes off into the hills to see Scarecrow. Sometimes to town. Sometimes... I don't know."

My mind runs wild again with ideas. He's gone...

"Let's get your feet bandaged and then we can figure out breakfast," Ember says with a warm smile. She appears as if she's aged overnight, but at the same time, her youthful joy is slowly returning. "I don't like you walking through the tunnel barefoot, but we'll clean them good in the bathroom."

When we get to the main house, we oddly both

head to the cellar rather than the main living area. I don't know if it's because we both worry Richard is still near and, in a way, we are hiding from him. Or maybe it has an odd feeling of safety and familiarity. Regardless of the reason, we go to the cellar and I carry my old chair of dignity to the bathroom and sit down so Ember can tend to me.

"There's so much dried blood, that it's hard to see," she says as her brow furrows. She reaches for a lantern and matches and lights it so she can see better.

"I think they were surface cuts," I say, looking around the room, thinking.

Thinking.

I won't stop thinking until we are out of here.

She opens the medicine cabinet and pulls out peroxide and bandages. The sight of blood doesn't seem to bother her which fascinates me. Although after what we both watched last night, a few bloody cuts on the bottom of a man's feet seems like child's play.

She reaches for the handle in the shower and starts the water. "I think it's best for you to shower and really get the feet clean," she directs. "Do you want me to wash your clothes again?"

I shake my head. "You just did."

I know she wants to keep busy. My mother always tried to keep busy too after Dad's death. I recognize this tactic. But I do get up, undress and get into the shower to rinse off all the blood, the dirt, and the memories of the mill. Ember has to stand right next to the shower with only the curtain separating us due to the chain. It's how we've showered up until this point, which seems silly, but I respect her discomfort with nudity and being near me in that way.

"What about you?" I call out as I begin to lather up with soap. "A shower might make you feel a lot better too."

I'm surprised when the shower curtain is pushed to the side and a naked Ember joins me under the stream of water.

"Hold me," she says. "I just want to forget that yesterday even happened." She looks up into my eyes and brings her lips to mine. "Help me forget."

I'm taken aback by her boldness, but I do exactly as she asks. I move her body so that she is in the stream of water completely. If there is a way to wash away our misery, I would. She presses her forehead to my chest and releases a shaky breath.

"I want to leave here," she says. "I want to leave and never look back again."

Words I had been waiting to hear.

Finally... finally...

"Then we will," I say as I tighten my hold on her as warm water covers our bodies in a cascade of hope.

"You won't leave me?"

"Never," I say as I tilt her face up to me and press my lips to hers.

My body becomes alive, and I realize I need her as much as she does me to forget. For a moment in time, I need to just feel comfort and hope.

I run circles along her heated flesh, dipping my hand lower between her legs. My fingers run along her silky folds, spreading signs of her arousal all over her pussy, mixing with the stream of water from the showerhead. She attempts to clamp her legs together to conceal her arousal.

I nudge her thighs wider with my hand. I dip my finger back to her soaking pussy, move my finger to her clit, and caress it ever so gently.

Ember tenses and looks at me with wide eyes. The hunger in her eyes nearly changes her appearance. From innocent and afraid, to sexual vixen in seconds.

"Do you like that?" I ask.

She nods and then places her head on my chest again as she moans out in pleasure as I continue to massage her clit.

Heat radiates off her body, and my cock throbs in need.

Leaning down and kissing her lips, I murmur against them, "I need to be inside you."

I flip her around and press her palms against the wall of the shower. I spread her legs and pull her hips out so her ass is on full display for my viewing. I consider that I may be being a tad too aggressive or harsh for her still sexual inexperience, but I can't help myself. My own needs take over, and like she said to me... I need to forget as well. Right now, I want to think of nothing more than being with this woman. I want to pretend that we aren't in a cellar. That we aren't chained together. I want to block out the Hell that I am in and focus on the only shining beacon I've had this entire time.

Taking hold of my cock, I guide it to her pussy and press in with one thrust. I pause when I'm buried balls deep inside of her so we can both adjust to the sensation. She gasps and her breathing increases in speed, and I love watching her delicate fingers splayed against the tile.

Not being able to control my urge to fuck her hard, I begin doing exactly that. Over and over, I pound into her. I wrap my arm around her waist, pulling her into me, and I use the other hand to support my weight against the wall.

"Yes," she pants as tiny moans blend with the sound of the shower cascading around us.

Her pussy is tight around me, and I know I'm spreading her wide with every forceful drive of my cock.

"Release," I command as I push even deeper, hearing her mewls intensify.

Being the perfect obedient wife, I feel her body

tense beneath me, and the walls of her sex tighten around my dick. She presses her forehead to the tile and cries out as her body nearly vibrates against mine.

It's all I need to feel my own orgasm near. Pumping in and out a few more times, I take hold of my cock and pull out as I shoot come all over her ass. Not wasting a second, I spin her around, kiss her with the same desire that demanded I take her, and I hold her in my arms as I rinse her body from my passion.

"I love you, Christopher," she says as she looks up at me, eyelashes fluttering, and with blue eyes I can get lost in.

I tighten my hold of her and kiss her on the top of the head. "I love you. I don't know what the future looks like, but I'm never going to let you go."

"I won't ever let you go." I feel her thin arms squeeze around my waist, and I know she means every single word.

What does our future look like?

I have no idea.

Are we to be trapped for the rest of our lives in this prison? Will there now be two ghosts of Hallelujah Junction? Will I become folklore as well?

A husband and wife forever bound in love in the afterlife.

Stories will be told. Sightings will occur. A man

and a wife side by side staring out of the schoolhouse to the people below.

Is this my future?

I don't want to be a ghost. I want to pull Ember from the underworld and bring her back to life. I want a life. A real life for the two of us. A renewed energy surges through me. I'll save us. *We* will save us.

"Papa Rich is gone," I say to Christopher as I stare out the kitchen window. "I see his snowshoe tracks leading up to the hills. He's off to see Scarecrow and pray. He does this after he feels he's... gone too far."

Christopher leans over my shoulder to see for himself. "Where does Scarecrow live?"

"I've only been to Scarecrow's place once. It's far up in the hills. There was once another mining town that barely stands that he calls home. He lives in an old church that he's made his home. It's one of the few buildings that are left standing. The other structures have really been abused by the elements and aren't inhabitable. Not that Scarecrow would want to have neighbors. He likes to live out there by himself. Although he is on the hunt for a wife."

"Jesus, how many mining towns are there?"

I chuckle. "A lot actually. They are splattered through the Nevada hills and desert and go into California. Some are preserved by the states and some aren't."

"How long is he usually gone when he goes and visits Scarecrow? Are we talking hours? Days?" Christopher pushes.

"He'll be gone all day for sure. Papa Rich rarely spends the night there. If weather comes in, maybe…"

Christopher spins me around so I have to look at him. "Ember, did you mean it when you said you want to leave?"

My heart skips and nausea rolls through my stomach. I nod slowly. "Yes, but… I can't bear another consequence if we do something foolish and get caught."

"We have to try to get out of here. This may be our only chance," he says as he glances out the window again. "Can you show me his room?"

That request seems simple and harmless enough. What Papa Rich doesn't know…

I lead us down the narrow hallway and stop before his door. There is a split second I consider turning us around. I'm so programmed to obey and do nothing against my father, and yet, with Christopher by my side, I feel I can break the rule of never entering his room.

I turn the door handle with shaky hands and the door opens. It's the first time I've seen his room in all my life. This is his special place. His sanctuary. I'm invading his space, and I begin to panic.

"What if he knows? He always knows," I say with a weak voice as my knees begin to tremble. I yank on Christopher's arm. "There's nothing in here we need. Let's go."

"I only need a couple of minutes to look around."

I see his single bed which is nicely made. The rest of the furnishings are basic. There is a dresser, a nightstand and a chair. No paintings, no decorations, nothing that makes the room special. But Papa Rich never believed in materialistic things.

Riches are the root to evil.

"We're going to be gone before he returns," Christopher announces as he leads the charge into the room. "He won't ever know we were in here."

Christopher goes straight to the closet door and opens it. The first thing we see is Papa's ranger uniforms hanging nicely in a row. No other clothes are hanging with them. Christopher smiles when he looks to the ground and sees a pair of hiking boots, and my goloshes that I got to wear when Papa and I went snowshoeing together before... well... before he stole Christopher. He picks them up, hands me my shoes, and leads us back to the chair and sits down and starts putting the hiking boots on.

"They're tight, but better than nothing." Christopher's smile grows. "He fucked up. He really didn't think before he left. Did he really think we'd do nothing?"

I can now see what Christopher is thinking. He plans to have us try to hike out of here again, but at least this time we won't be barefoot.

"It's far," I say. "Even with shoes, we may not get out of here and into town before he returns and hunts us down with the ranger truck." I'm not just telling this to Christopher out of fear, but out of reason. Christopher has underestimated my father before, and I refuse to let that happen again.

Christopher moves on as if I didn't say a single word. He helps me put on my boots and then turns his attention to the dresser. He begins pulling out clothing in search for something warm. Satisfied when he finds some sweaters, he quickly pulls one over his head and then dresses me in one as well which dwarfs my body in wool.

"Do you think he has coats anywhere?"

"There's a hall closet with his ranger coats. I'm sure he has his thick one on now for his hike." I know he has a rain coat and a lighter jacket as well.

Christopher reaches for the quilt on the bed

and pulls it off. He bundles it in his arms and leads us out of the room.

"Even if we are warm enough," I begin. "It's about how much time we have. It will take us hours to get down the hill. We will be racing against the time it takes for him to return and him jumping in the truck. You know he'll come after us."

"What about the truck?" Christopher asks. The mention of the truck only fuels his exit plan ideas more. "Is there any way we can find his keys?"

"He'd not leave the keys. He isn't that stupid," I say, not even having to look to see. Although I point to a drawer. "If they are anywhere, they are in that drawer."

Christopher nearly has us sprinting to see, and I watch his face fall as he finds the drawer empty as I expected.

I look outside and see that it's snowing again. The thought of hiking down a hill to the town is daunting. Especially chained together. We struggle to walk comfortably, let alone try to run while shackled. In fact, it feels near impossible. It will be cold. We can die of hyperthermia, shoes or not. And if we get caught...

Papa Rich will torture Christopher right in front of my eyes. He can't take anything more from me now that Pine Cone is gone, but he can kill Christopher. He can make me live the rest of my life without him. I also know that Papa Rich will make me marry Scarecrow as my penance, and I prefer to die in the acid pit over that.

"I think we need to think this through," I begin.

Christopher takes my hand and brushes my hair away from my face. "I know you're afraid. I know warning bells are going off in your head, but I need you to trust me. I need you to give your all. We can escape here if we stick to my plan. I need you not to fight me. I need you to work with me on this. We'll be free, Ember. I swear to you, we will be."

I want to do what Christopher asks. I want to be a good wife. But more than that, I want to be free.

Yes, free.

I don't even know what that word really means. Away from Papa Rich, I suppose means free. Not having to ever see Scarecrow again means free. Leaving Hallelujah Junction and not having to walk amongst the tunnels or be forever locked in a schoolhouse would be free.

But then what?

Where will I live? What will I do?

Who will I be?

Will I be Ember the Hallelujah Junction ghost forever?

I don't know what the world looks like. I don't know what people will say or do. I don't know how to live and breathe in another world. I may be in a cage now like an animal, but I'm fed, I'm protected...

"My mother," I say to Christopher. "If I leave here, who will protect me from my mother? She could find out I'm alive and where to find me. Papa Rich warned me that leaving here means she can find me."

Christopher places his palms on both sides of my face and stares at me in the eyes. "It's a story," he begins. "Richard made this up to scare you and to explain why he would never let you leave this town. The real reason he keeps you hidden from the world is because he'd go to jail if anyone found out about you. You aren't his. You never were. He kidnapped you, Ember. He kept you locked here in his own manipulative way. I know that's hard to hear, but it's the truth. He stole you."

I shake my head, not wanting to hear the words that deep down I know to be true.

"Why?" I swallow hard and divert my eyes from Christopher's stare. "Why would he do that to me? Why would he want to keep me locked up? He's my father. He loves me."

"Ember..." Christopher leans forward and kisses my forehead and then embraces me. "He's a sick man. I can't give you a reason for why he does what he does. He's killed people. Only monsters and demons kill people. He's not your father. He's nothing but darkness, and you have to escape that. You believe we have to get away, right?"

I nod against his chest. "Yes."

I begin to cry, and I don't know why. Is it because I'm scared? Is it because I'm leaving Papa Rich and it's breaking my heart thinking about what I will do without him? Am I sick like him because a part of me doesn't want to leave? Part of me wants to stay... why?

But the sane part of me screams to my soul. I know we have to leave. Not just because of my freedom but because of Christopher's. He can't spend the rest of his life chained to me in a place that isn't his home.

This isn't right. It's never been right.

"And if by some chance," Christopher adds, "you do have some crazy mother out there who wants to harm you, I'll protect you with my life. You have nothing to worry about."

"Then we should go," I say with a sudden spike of courage. "If we try to run, we may beat him before he returns."

24

CHRISTOPHER

EMBER'S RIGHT. WE CAN TRY TO RUN AS FAST AS WE can in the snow, but it will take time. Time we might not have. And I can't risk us being caught again. This is our one shot, and if I don't plan this out perfectly, then Richard will win again. I can't have that happen.

"We need the authorities to come to us," I say.

"I told you there is no phone or radio. Well there is, but I know Richard has that on him," Ember says.

I freeze for a second realizing that Ember has called her Papa Rich by his full name. She's morphing before my eyes. Courage looks good on her, and I've never been prouder. I know this can't be easy for her. I can't imagine how terrified she must be. And not just because of the fear of being caught. But I also know she's afraid of what happens if we actually do escape. She has no idea what awaits her on the other side.

And her thoughts are valid.

Can Ember survive in the world I live? This is a girl who has never worn shoes or watched television. Electronics and the Internet don't exist in her mind. She doesn't know what it's like to have the constant buzz of sound in her ears from city life. She doesn't even know what a city is. I'm the third person in her life she has ever spoken to since she was taken. She's been a caged bird that has been raised in captivity. Is it fair to throw her out to the wild?

She has no idea what modern society is like, and I'm about to toss her into the lion's den if we do manage to escape. The thought of what happens next for Ember is almost as terrifying as Richard finding and stopping us.

We will be free from the evil of Richard, but not necessarily free from evil in general. The world is hard and brutal at times, and it can chew up a normal human being. But Ember... she's different. She's fragile. And the world could engulf her. Life could be harder for her outside this town than it is inside it, but no matter how hard, anything is better than the hell of Hallelujah Junction.

"I have an idea that is going to help us," I say. "We will bring the authorities to us."

I lead us down to the cellar where we have left

the lantern still lit. I pick it up and look at the small flame, knowing exactly what I have to do. Ember looks at me with confusion.

"We're going to catch the town on fire before we leave," I say, reaching for the matches as well.

"What? No. We can't." Ember tugs at my arm and shakes her head furiously. "It's been here for decades. Long before us. We can't burn it. The history... we can't. It's my home."

"It's not your home." I try to take a deep breath and soften my voice. I know I have to be gentle with Ember even if I grow frustrated. I have to put myself in her situation, but at the same time, I know we are running against the clock.

"Christopher, I don't—"

"We have no other choice," I defend. "You're right in saying that Richard might reach us before we get all the way to town. But if the authorities see the smoke and come, they will meet us halfway down the hill. They will get to us before Richard. The fire will be our own S.O.S."

"But if he sees the smoke before he reaches Scarecrow, he may return quicker than planned," she points out.

I pause and consider her words. "True. But it's a risk we have to take."

Not wanting to wait another second, I take the lantern over to the pile of dirty blankets that I spent my first week sleeping on. It will be therapeutic in a twisted way to watch the soiled material burn. The cellar should be the first place in this town to burn to the ground.

When they ignite almost immediately, I know we have crossed the line of no return. I lead us to the bathroom and yank the bottle of rubbing alcohol out of the medicine cabinet and begin splattering it all over the floor to help aid the flames in mastering the room.

We both stand for several minutes and watch the blankets burn and the fire spread across the floorboards, making its way to the wooden crates. I know that once the flames lick the wood, it won't be long until the fire takes over completely.

Taking Ember by the hand, I lead us upstairs to the kitchen to grab the quilt and the coats Ember pulled out of the closet. I put the heaviest coat on her and then also wrap her tiny frame in the quilt. I pray she will be warm enough. We don't have to last long... just until help comes from the fire department.

I also grab the bottle of Jack Daniels that Richard bought me to help ignite the fires I will set. Once we have everything in hand, I turn on the gas stove and allow the gas to run without a flame. It will help ignite the fire even more when it reaches the kitchen.

"I'm hoping there's a sprinkler system on the

buildings below," I say, thinking that there may be in some of the buildings.

I'm pretty sure the Forest Department would want that, but then if that is the case, there may also be automatic fire alarms that go straight to a company notifying of a fire emergency. Either way, my intent is to start them all aflame. But first... the fucking mill must burn to the ground.

It's easier to walk to the mill wearing shoes, even if they are so tight that they border on painful, but at least my feet aren't freezing in the snow.

"I don't want to go back there," Ember says, tugging on my arm and stopping in her tracks. "I don't want to go anywhere near it."

I don't blame her, but this is still something I feel I must do. "Only for a second," I say with the lantern in my hand. "We're burning the fucker from existence."

She nibbles her lower lip and stares ahead as if seeing ghosts I can't see. Knowing how painful it was for me to watch that couple die in the most gory and disgusting way, I can only imagine all the memories Ember must have of the mill. She had to watch death after death of innocent people, not to mention her precious cat. I'm sure she wants to see it forever vanish from her mind as well.

"We need to do it for all who died there," I say. "It needs to never exist again."

Appearing satisfied with my answer, she

continues on toward the mill. When we get there, I smell sulfur and other minerals, but I also feel I smell death.

The mill is the shallow grave of many, and it reeks of their sizzled bones. If there is an entrance to hell, then this mill is it, and I feel it my duty to burn it to the ground and allow the poor souls to rest in peace with their ashes being all that remains.

I notice a piece of wood that I feel I can use as a torch that I can light and then throw into the building without having to actually go inside. I agree with Ember on not wanting to have to see the inside of the gut of the Devil again. I don't want to risk seeing the ghosts of the couple who had wanted to help us. I don't want to see their eyes looking at me, accusing me of causing their deaths. I don't want to hear the howls of their misery as the sounds forever haunt the mill.

Tossing the lit torch inside, and then lighting all the spare wood on the outside of the mill, Ember and I stand hand in hand as the structure lights. I take a swig of the last of the Jack in celebration of seeing this building ignite. My face heats from the fire, and I know we must move on to another building. As much as I would like to stand before it and watch it melt before me, I know we have little time.

As we walk to the schoolhouse, Ember shakes

her head. "Burn down all the other buildings. But not that one. Leave that one."

I don't want to leave a single building of this awful town. I want nothing but charred earth when done, but I have to take Ember's feelings into consideration. This isn't just about me. It's about her. This nightmare is one she has lived her entire life and if anyone gets to make the call, it's her.

I squeeze her hand that I haven't released and agree. I tighten the quilt around her to try to ease the shivers I see wrack her body. "If that's what you want."

"I don't want to see it die. Not because of me. It deserves to stand on that hill. It was my safe place. It protected me. I need to protect it now."

We make our way to the other buildings that are part of the tourist section. I look over my shoulder and see the main house is completely engulfed in flames, and the mill is as well. I have never seen a more morbid and beautiful sight in my life. Even if Richard catches us... there will be no Hallelujah Junction to return to. Nothing but ash. Nothing but embers. Nothing but the ghosts with no place to call their own any longer.

The old wood lights up fast, and I'm pleased to see that the ranger's office appears to be hardwired to an alarm. My hope is that by now, the authorities have been notified of a fire, and help is coming.

"Oh my God," Ember screams as she points up toward the mill. "He's coming! Richard is coming!"

I snap my head in the direction she's pointing and see Richard running as fast as he can in his snowshoes down the hill. His strides are wide, and his arms propel him faster down the hill than I think is possible. His body charges forward with a mission to save, with a goal to capture his prey, and a determination to be victorious.

He's watching everything that has ever meant a thing to him go up in flames. He has to witness it all disappear before him.

I warned him that I would see his world burn.

Burn.

Burn!

By God I am burning it all to the fucking ground.

He's still a distance from us, and I know if we act fast, we can still get away. I also know it's likely he has his pistol on him, and after what he sees we are doing to his precious town, he will no doubt aim the gun right between my eyes and pull the trigger.

I still have the lantern with me, and I run Ember and me toward his truck which is parked by the ranger's office. I don't want to wait for the flames to reach the truck on their own in case Richard gets to the vehicle before they do. I decide I need to speed up the process. I run to the gas tank and open it. I then rip a piece of fabric from the hem of Ember's dress and stick it in. I then pull out the gas-soaked material, stick in the clean side, and then light it.

Not waiting to see the truck light, and concerned it could explode, I take Ember by the hand. "Run. Run as fast as you can. He's coming, but he's not going to catch us."

I've already decided in my mind that if he does catch up with us, I will fight to my death. I will strangle the man to death if I have to. I will kill him at whatever cost.

I can hear the fire burning behind us, and with a quick glance over my shoulder, I see the truck light up in flames. Now it will be a matter of if Richard can outrun us. Yes, we are chained together, but we have a head start. He's still a ways away from the mill, and he has a long distance to even get where we are.

"Run!"

Ember and I begin hobbling side by side as if we are running a potato-sack race. Step after step, we make our way out of the burning town. When we hit the parking lot, I pause just enough to see if I can view where Richard is. I see him run into the main house, and by the sudden stop of our run, Ember must see the same thing.

"No! He's going inside! The fire! It will burn him alive," she screams.

I have no idea why he's running inside the burning building. Maybe to get the pistol I incorrectly assumed he was carrying. Maybe there is something valuable inside he can't live without. Maybe he thinks he can save it.

It's Ember...

He doesn't see us. He doesn't know Ember is outside on the run.

He thinks she's inside burning to death, or at least could be. He's running into the burning building to save his daughter. He'll die to save her. He won't allow her to die.

Monster or not... he's still a father.

And because of that... the flames with swallow him whole.

"Christopher! He's going to die in there."

There's nothing we can do, and even if we could, I won't. I know I can't allow Ember to break down now or try to foolishly insist we return to help.

"Don't look. Run," I order, and thank God, she obeys.

I can only imagine what watching the only world she has ever known burn around her is doing to her sanity. But Richard can emerge from the fire any second and catch up to us. "We need to keep running, Ember. Run. Our lives depend on it."

The mill is collapsing, the main house with the cellar underneath is completely engulfed, and the rest of the town is turning into an inferno. It won't be long until nothing is left at all. But the schoolhouse... the schoolhouse on the top of the hill remains untouched. The only thing different about the schoolhouse is that the ghost of Hallelujah Junction is no longer inside. She's beside me. She's my captive bride. She's mine and will never return to her eternal damnation.

Ember looks over her shoulder again, hesitates for a moment, but then allows me to tug her forward. I see tears running down her face, and my heart breaks for her.

We run down the hill with every last bit of energy we have. I feel evil breathing down my neck, but I plow forward. I know the Devil is reaching out with his claws to pull us back in, but I refuse to let it happen. I don't look back in fear of what I will see.

I just hold on to Ember and emerge from the flames.

The snow bites at our faces, and yet we power on. With my wife by my side, I know we are close. We are so close to breaking free. One foot after another.

One foot after another.

Goodbye Devil... goodbye Hell...

"What is that sound?" Ember asks, still running as fast as she possibly can.

"Our future, Ember. That's the sound of our future."

Click here for KEPT BRIDE.

Thank you for taking the time to read all about Ember and Christopher. But their story doesn't stop yet. The Secret Bride Trilogy follows them in the next two books, KEPT BRIDE and TAKEN BRIDE. I hope you continue on with their journey.

THE SECRET BRIDE SERIES

<u>CAPTIVE BRIDE:</u>

You will take this bride.

To have and to hold from this day forward.

Till death do you part.

This will be your solemn vow.

You have no choice.

Trapped in a twisted and dark courtship with a secret woman who needs my strength to survive, I will be wed.

Walking the thin line between lunacy and reality, I am now the protector of my future captive bride.

So, I have no choice but to recite the vows.

I take thee.

In this arranged matrimony.

Until we are parted by death.

<u>KEPT BRIDE:</u>

My history is forbidden.

My story, dark and twisted.

My future decided.

I know I don't belong in this decadent world—his world.

Money, power, and dark secrets surround me now.

I submit to it all to be his perfect obedient wife.

They stalk my every move, watching me, judging me.

I'm in the same prison just with different guards.

But all I care about is him.

His eyes, his touch, his hold over me.

I'm forever his kept bride, even though they all try to steal me away.

TAKEN BRIDE:

Secrets must be kept.

Vows never broken.

Till death do us part...

Unless everything changes.

Captive in one life...

Kept in another...

Taken to now be the wife I am forced to be.

I'm hidden away to face a dark reality only a few can survive.

But I have a purpose now. I can be the good wife I strive to be.

But he still wants me.

He will hunt me down.

He will find me and take back what was stolen.

I will be his wife if he has to fight until the death to make it happen.

ALSO BY ALTA HENSLEY

Breaking Belles Series:

Elegant Sins

Beautiful Lies

Opulent Obsession

Inherited Malice

Delicate Revenge

Lavish Corruption

———

Kings & Sinners Series:

Maddox

Stryder

Anson

———

Dark Fantasy Series:

Snow & the Seven Huntsmen

Red & the Wolves

Queen & the Kingsmen

———

Captive Vow

Spiked Roses

Prima

Mr. D

Mafia Lullaby

Naughty Girl

Bride to Keep

Delicate Scars

Bad Bad Girl

His Caged Kitty

Bared

Caged

Forbidden

ABOUT ALTA HENSLEY

Alta Hensley is a USA TODAY bestselling author of hot, dark and dirty romance. She is also an Amazon Top 100 bestselling author. Being a multi-published author in the romance genre, Alta is known for her dark, gritty alpha heroes, sometimes sweet love stories, hot eroticism, and engaging tales of the constant struggle between dominance and submission.

As a gift for being my reader, I would like to offer you a FREE book.

DELICATE SCARS

Get your copy now! ~
https://dl.bookfunnel.com/tnpuad5675

I was going to ruin her.

I knew it the moment I laid eyes on her. She was too naive, too innocent.

I would wrap her in the darkness of my world till she no longer craved the light... only me.

I should walk away, leave her clean and untouched... but I won't.

I hold her delicate heart in my scarred fist and I have no intention of letting go.

It all started with a book... doesn't that sound crazy?

For your entire world to come crashing down around you over research for a book?

But that is what it felt like the moment I met him.

My world tilted. Nothing made sense any more.

I only know he became like a drug to me... and I shook with need till my next fix.

Join Alta's Facebook Group for Readers for access to deleted scenes, to chat with me and other fans and also get access to exclusive giveaways:
Alta's Private Facebook Room

Check out Alta Hensley:
Website: www.altahensley.com
Facebook: facebook.com/AltaHensleyAuthor
Twitter: twitter.com/AltaHensley
Instagram: instagram.com/altahensley
BookBub: bookbub.com/authors/alta-hensley
Sign up for Alta's Newsletter: readerlinks. com/l/727720/nl

SNEAK PEEK

What do you think of Papa Rich?

Would you like to get a sneak peek of where The Secret Bride Series all began? Richard plays a part in a book I wrote a few years ago called CAPTIVE VOW. Let's just say that he learned all his wicked ways from the best.

CAPTIVE VOW

CHAPTER ONE

Jack and Jill went up the hill to fetch a pail of water.

> *Jack fell down and broke his crown,*
> *And Jill came tumbling after.*

My momma used to hum that nursery rhyme. She used to hum it a lot. And on days she was stressed, anxious, or short fused, she would even sing it with a high-pitched, haunting voice over and over again like a stuck record. It was the sound of my childhood. I hated that song.

I still remember the day I asked her why she loved it so. I wanted to know why two people climbing a hill and then falling off it was so important to her. Who was Jack? Who was Jill? She had looked at me stunned, as if surprised I had noticed and had paid attention to her humming and singing it all these years. Or was she shocked I didn't know the answer to my question? Whatever it was, she studied me for several minutes before answering me.

"It was your father's and my song. It reflects us. Our love we once shared."

My mother never spoke of my father. I had never met him nor ever saw a picture. Whenever I asked about him, for stories describing who he was, my momma was quick to shut it down. She said he was 'gone' and that was the best answer I would ever get.

"A nursery rhyme?" I had asked. "*That* was your song?"

"Yes. It's about two lovers who beat all the odds holding them down. They climb above it all, but only to be crushed again."

"I don't understand. Why do they have a pail of water?"

"A pail of water is a euphemism for having sex. For finally being in love and able to be together. But then Jack dies... and Jill soon follows."

"They die?"

She nodded, appearing so deep in thought. "Yes, they both eventually die."

The sound of the phone ringing in the middle of the night was never a good thing. It's always the sound of bad news, an emergency, or even death. The shrill resonance cutting through the night's air is like a town crier announcing impending doom.

My heart thumped against my chest as I reached for my cell phone sitting on the nightstand beside my bed. The number on the screen showed unknown, which only intensified my panic.

I cleared my throat, not wanting to sound as if I had been woken from a deep slumber and answered, "Hello?"

There was an operator's voice on the other end. "This is a collect call for Demi Wayne from The Eastland Women's Correction Facility. Would you like to accept the charges?" I had heard this question many times before.

"Yes, I will accept the charges." I sat up in my bed and turned on the bedside lamp, rubbing the sleep out of my eyes.

A clicking sound was followed by, "Demi?"

"Hello." I felt sick. I wanted to vomit. Her voice on the other end always made me feel ill, but tonight was worse. So much worse. I scanned my nightstand, wishing I still had the emergency pack of cigarettes I kept for an occasion such as this. Why the fuck did I decide to quit?

"How are you?" she asked.

What did she expect me to say? How was I supposed to be when I was getting a call from my mother in the middle of the night from a prison where she'd been incarcerated for the past six years? I needed a goddamn cigarette is how I was.

"Fine," I lied.

"Have you been watching the news?"

"No." Ever since my mother was arrested for blowing up a building and killing the five guards on that night's duty, I avoided the media completely. I couldn't take it. The pictures of her. The pictures of me. The pictures of us together and how the media would say I was a spitting image of my mother. They would say we looked like angels with our blonde hair and blue eyes, but then in the same sentence, say my mother had nothing but the devil inside of her. I didn't want to look like her. I didn't want to be the devil. I hated the media. I hated them all. I couldn't handle all the awful things being said about my mother.

Demon.

Murderer.

Monster.

And they were all true. Everything they said was true.

There was a long pause of silence. "I'm calling to say goodbye," she said with a wavering voice.

Bile built up in the back of my throat. "Goodbye?" We had already said our goodbyes when she was handcuffed and escorted off to prison. So what could she possibly mean by saying it again?

"I lost the final appeal."

I remained silent. I struggled to comprehend the information being fed through the phone line. It was as if my body was protecting me from processing the words threatening to shatter my soul. *Lost. Final.*

"I'm being sentenced to death tomorrow. Lethal injection. The lawyer says today was my final attempt at overturning the guilty verdict. I lost again."

Guilty.

The judge and jury had deemed her guilty.

She *was* guilty. She had placed the bomb in the building. She had killed those men. When she was asked why, she had said it was for the cause. The company housed in the building was testing against animals. *She* had been the judge and jury in that case, deciding that the experiments they were conducting deemed them worthy of being destroyed. 'A cause,' she had stated over and over. She was proud of her cause. She was proud of what she did. Not once did she say she was sorry. Not once did she glance over at the wives and families of the men she killed and beg for their forgiveness. Not once did she look at me and tell me she had made a huge mistake and wished she could take it all back. Not once did she show even an ounce of decency in her actions. When I had asked her why she would kill those innocent men, praying to God it was an accident, she simply shrugged and told me it was collateral damage. The price to pay for a bigger and better cause. So yes, what the media was saying about her was true.

Demon.

Murderer.

Monster.

My momma.

Yes.

So, I had no choice but to carry the shame for the both of us, and what a heavy weight it was. On my eighteenth birthday, I sat in the crowded courtroom and watched my mother stand with an aura of defiance and pride while the judge sentenced her to death for five counts of murder.

Happy Birthday to me.

"Demi?"

"Yes?" My voice cracked. I glanced around my bedroom at the piles of dirty clothes strewn about as my heart threatened to beat out of my chest. My room reflected my life. Dirty, neglected, disarrayed, shambles. My life was in chaos, and all I wanted right now was a fucking cigarette. This couldn't be real. This couldn't be real. This couldn't be real... yet, it was.

"Did you hear what I said?"

"Yes."

There was a long pause as darkness suffocated me. As darkness stabbed at my heart over and over. As darkness bludgeoned me to a bloody pulp. Darkness destroyed me as I sat there with the phone to my ear.

Dead man walking...

Correction.

Dead *woman* walking...

"It's okay, Demi. I'm at peace. I finally get to be with your father."

I said nothing as I struggled to breathe. The small room of my one-bedroom apartment shrank in size as the walls appeared to be closing in on me. I was trapped in this nightmare that I couldn't elude. There was no escape from my life.

"*Jack and Jill went up the hill to fetch a pail of water. Jack fell down and broke his crown. And Jill came tumbling after,*" she sang softly as she had done so many times in my youth. She paused, as if she were waiting for me to say something. As if wanting me to ask for clarification.

I wanted to scream for her to stop. I didn't want to hear that awful nursery rhyme ever again. I wanted her to shut the fuck up! Yet, I didn't want those to be my last words to her. No matter what, she didn't deserve that. I didn't want her to die hearing my cruel—but honest—words ringing in her ears. A daughter's truth to a mother who had done her wrong... so very wrong. So, I remained silent. Silent like all the times I watched her and others meet in my living room planning to take down a government agency or corrupt company. These strangers plotting and planning in my childhood home all spoke as if they were the good guys, and everyone else were the villains. I had grown up to distrust our government due to all the conspiracy theories I heard growing up. I never questioned. I never disagreed. I never told a soul of their plans. I only remained silent as a good little girl would do.

"I'm proud. Your father died for his cause, and now I get to tumble down after him."

I had finally learned all about my father after my mother was arrested. Not from my momma, but by the television. The media had informed me that my father—who I was simply told was 'gone'—had died in a blaze of police gunfire when he refused to surrender after trying to blow up a nuclear power plant. He was a leader of a terrorist group. He had died that day, leaving behind a grieving widow and a three-month-old baby. I can still remember the news anchor who stared into the camera while video of my father played behind his profile. The anchorman's gray hair, perfect suit and blue-striped tie, his firm, emotionless expression as he spoke into the camera were still so clear in my memory. Did he know that behind his head on the television screen was a gruesome image playing of a man losing his life as he was gunned down? A man who was my father? Did the news anchor have any idea there was a young woman watching her father—who she knew nothing about—for the first time while he died on old video footage? I often wonder if that news anchor had any idea a piece of me died that day. I had to meet my father, watch them describe my mother as the devil, and come to terms with the fact that I was nothing but an orphan with a dark and twisted family tree. I was a fool. Fooled by my past.

"When?" I asked, swallowing the lump in the back of my throat. "When do you die?"

"They said two o'clock tomorrow."

Two o'clock.

Two o'clock and my mother would be dead.

How odd it must be to know the exact time you are going to die.

Was she afraid? I would be afraid.

The first hot tear fell from my eyes. "So this is it? The last time I get to talk to you?"

"Yes."

"Momma…" The rest of the tears followed as I slipped into a deep hole. At that moment, I wanted to be a little girl with her mother's soothing arms around her, comforting her, telling her it was all going to be okay. But nothing was going to be okay. Nothing at all.

"Promise me one thing," she said. "Promise me you'll find your Jack, and you will climb that hill. You deserve happiness and love. You deserve so much more than I was able to give you." She cleared her throat. "I have to go now."

Panic attacked. "Wait! Now?" Oh God! Was this the last time I would ever hear my mother's voice? Would these be our last words? "Is there anything we can do? Can we hold it off a little bit longer? Maybe hire another lawyer? Get a new judge? Anything? There has to be something!" I felt as if I was hanging on a cliff by my fingertips and the weight of my body was just too much. I was about to fall into the abyss.

"No. The time has finally come. Just know that though you may not have agreed with my cause or what I did, I at least stayed true to myself. True to what your father and I believed in. All I ask is you stay true to yourself, Demi."

"Momma..."

"Goodbye."

With a short metallic click, the phone went dead, and *Jill came tumbling after*.

Day of death. How do you start a day like that? Do you get up, shower, dress and go to work like any other day? How do you face the hours? The minutes? The seconds? How do you breathe when your soul is dying, but your body is too cruel to allow the sweet release of death? How does a daughter live as her mother prepares to die?

"Demi? Did you hear me?"

I turned to see Maria standing in the small break room, looking at me with concern. Her long black hair was set in a low bun like she always wore it while on shift, but the wayward hairs that framed her face revealed she had already worked several hours. The breakfast shift at *Blossoms Diner* could be a real bitch, and no doubt she was anxious to be relieved by me so she could go home and get some rest.

"What?" I hadn't even heard her come in, let alone say anything to me. Ever since the phone call, I felt as if I was wading through a dream cloaked in a thick fog.

"I asked if you were all right. You look a million miles away."

"Just a long night. I didn't get much sleep."

Maria was my friend—the only person I would really consider a friend—but I'd never told her about my mother. I hadn't told anyone about my mother. It wasn't exactly something I was proud of or wanted to relive by retelling the nightmare I tried desperately to keep locked away in the far corners of my mind. I had murderess blood that ran through my veins, and that was a secret I didn't want to reveal. Not to anyone.

Appearing satisfied with my lie, she said, "Story of my life. I swear, if Luis doesn't start sleeping through the night soon, I may die of sleep deprivation. He's just so darn cute that I can't help but pick him up from his crib. I know they say you are supposed to let them cry it out, but that just seems cruel to me."

I tried my best to give a smile and slight nod as I reached for my apron and tied it around my waist. Normally, I loved hearing stories of her sweet little baby, but the fog I was in nearly smothered me in despair. I was afraid Maria would know something was wrong by looking at me, as she always did. I just hoped today she'd write this one off as me being tired.

When I looked up at her after putting on my apron, I found her staring, appearing more concerned than before. "Hey, are you really okay? Are you sick or something? Do you want me to work your shift for you? I can call the sitter and have her stay longer. It's really not that big of a deal."

Having Maria work my shift would have been wonderful so I could just go crawl in bed and hide from all the emotions flooding me, but I didn't have the luxury. Missing even one shift meant me not being able to pay all my bills that month, and it was tight as it was.

I shook my head and gave the best reassuring smile I could give. "I'm fine. Once I get some coffee in me, I'll perk right up."

Maria seemed convinced with my answer, and she reached for the tie of her apron to remove it. "Table five is waiting for you."

"She's here today?"

"Every Tuesday and Thursday, and now Friday it seems. She's making a habit of eating here. Quite the regular. I already placed her order for her."

I let out a big sigh. Not that I minded our usual customer, in fact, she had become someone I actually cared for, but today I wasn't sure I had the patience or the ability to be kind to anyone. Viv Montgomery was a sweet old Asian lady with a heart of gold, but she did take a lot of my time and attention. "Any chance you can stay a bit longer? I know she'll need my help."

"Girl, you can't be expected to stop what you are doing and feed her every time she comes in."

Even though Maria said the words, I knew that if I didn't help Mrs. Montgomery eat her meal, Maria would most definitely step in and fill my shoes. She liked to play the hard ass, but I knew the real her. Maria wouldn't allow a little old lady to fend for herself, and I knew it.

Mrs. Montgomery had Parkinson's so bad, that

bringing a spoon to her lips by herself, usually left her covered in whatever food she ordered. Seeing the poor woman sitting alone in the diner's booth, shaking and struggling a few weeks back, I had taken it upon myself to help her. It was the least I could do. And the truth of the matter was, I enjoyed it. I liked the lady, and I liked the feeling that I was being of some use to someone in need.

"Just stay long enough for me to get her started. Can you cover me?"

Maria nodded with a tender smile as she went to put her apron back on. "Softie."

"Yeah, I guess I am," I said as I reached for a ponytail holder in my pocket and pulled my hair into a messy bun, preparing for another long day on my feet serving greasy food to patrons. Hopefully, I would be busy enough to keep my mind off of the nightmare in which I was imprisoned.

When I walked into the dining room, I went straight to table five where Mrs. Montgomery sat staring ahead. Her short grey hair rested on the top of her shoulders, curled to perfection, with tiny, pearl pins right above her ears. It was still possible to see the remnants of what must have been rich black hair in her youth. In this redneck, piece of shit town in South Carolina, an exotic, mature, beauty such as Vivian Montgomery was a rarity. I had also come to realize that she dressed up for her special lunches each and every time. She treated lunch at *Blossoms Diner* like someone would treat a meal at a fine dining establishment. She always wore a dress or skirt, shoes with a stubby heel, nude-colored pantyhose, and carried a different purse that matched her outfit each and every time. She never wore garish jewelry, but she would wear a strand of pearls or a necklace made of some type of semi-precious stone. Though her hands were covered in age spots and wrinkles, her nails were always painted a pretty pink or coral, manicured to perfection. It was obvious the woman took pride in her appearance, and wanted to be at her very best, even if it was for lunch in a small local diner.

"Mrs. Montgomery, don't you look marvelous today," I said as I placed the Cajun chicken pasta she had already ordered from Maria in front of her shaking hands and sat in the booth opposite to her.

She looked at me with the sweetest eyes and the warmest smile. "You are so kind, dear." She reached across to touch my hands that rested on the table. I could see she was shaking more than normal. She had told me that, with her Parkinson's, she had good days and bad days, but by the intensity of the tremors now, I would say she was having a bad day. I noticed the skin around her wrists looked raw and bruised. So, I made a mental note to ask her about it later, but didn't want to start off the meal by talking about her sickness and injuries due to it. "You look so pretty too."

I smirked, feeling anything but pretty. I couldn't remember if I had brushed my hair. The fact that I was even dressed was a feat within itself.

"Don't give me that look," she playfully scolded. "When I was your age, I envied women like you. Tall, big blue eyes, long light hair, and the perfect cherub face. Like a doll. You are such a lovely young lady."

I smiled and shook my head, feeling uncomfortable hearing her kind words. I never handled compliments very well.

"Thank you," I mumbled as I glanced over at Maria who was taking an order at one of the tables I was supposed to cover myself.

Mrs. Montgomery looked down at her meal and reached for her fork. I always allowed her to start, judging if she needed my help or not. She always did, but I would still watch for a short time to gauge how much. Today she could barely grab the fork, knocking the other silverware to the side as she struggled for the handle of the utensil.

Without asking, I took the fork and poked it into a piece of pasta and chicken. "Why don't I help you with that?"

She nodded and smiled. Her eyes made contact with mine, and we connected like we had done many times before. "Thank you. I don't know what I would do without you."

I fed her the food and returned the smile, poking the pasta for the second bite. "And I don't know what I would do without you, Mrs. Montgomery. You are the sunshine to my day."

"I wish you would call me Viv," she said as she finished the bite of her food. She then took another bite the minute she was done chewing, her entire body quivering lightly as she did so.

"I was taught by my momma to always address my elders in the proper fashion." I gave her a wink, trying to hide the stab in my heart which occurred by bringing up my mother.

Fuck! Why did I say that? I didn't want to think about her. I didn't want to remember a single thing. I just wanted to feed this nice woman and go about my day. One meal, one hour, one minute at a time, and I would survive this day. I had to survive the day my mother would die.

"You must have had a very good momma. She has taught you to be a kind and generous woman." Mrs. Montgomery continued to eat, opening her mouth in a child-like fashion each time I brought the food to her lips.

A dull ache attacked my head, and a ringing filled my ears. I didn't want to talk about my momma. No, she was not a good momma. A good momma would not have done what she did. A

good momma would not have left her child to fend
off the cruel world by herself. A good momma
would not die for a cause that did not matter. I did
not have a good momma. I did not have a good
momma at all.

"But I still wish you would call me Viv. Friends
should be on a first name basis; don't you think?"

Trying to snap out of the spiraling fall from the
cliff where I was so precariously balanced, I gave a
smirk. "I suppose you are right. We are friends, and
we should call each other by our first names. But
that goes for you as well then. You call me Demi."
She had only called me 'dear' since we first met.

Feeding Viv another bite, I noticed her eyes
seemed to glisten as if she were struggling holding
back tears. "I don't have any friends," she said.

"Oh, I'm sure you have friends."

She shook her head. "No."

I placed the fork down on the plate, reached for
her glass of water, and helped her drink from it.
"Well, I'll let you in on a little secret. Other than
Maria who works here, I don't have any friends
either. I pretty much keep to myself." I picked up
the fork and once again stabbed at a piece of spiced
chicken. "And the truth is, I often am suspicious of
people who have lots and lots of friends. I mean,
how can you be best friends with everyone? I think
it's impossible. There's only so much of your heart
you can give. I would much rather give more of me

—the real me—to those select and special people than just a little of me to a large group simply so I can say I have a lot of friends."

Viv turned her head to look at Maria who was behind the counter getting drinks ready. "And Maria is your friend?" she asked.

"Yes. She's really nice and fun to work with. She has a new baby who is just about the cutest thing you've ever seen. We both don't have any family around, so we spend the holidays together... so, I guess you could say we are more than friends."

She looked surprised. "No family?"

I shook my head, hoping to God she would drop the subject. I was not going to go into my awful situation with her or anyone. "No."

"And you don't have a special person in your life?" she asked as she reached for her napkin to wipe at some white cream sauce that stuck to the corner of her lip. Her hand shook the entire time, but she had managed to do it herself.

I shrugged. "Not interested in having a someone special right now."

"Why?"

I didn't usually like talking about myself to anyone, but this little old lady and I had spent many hours chatting as I fed her. I felt comfortable talking to her which was odd, but, at the same time, I liked it.

"All the good ones are taken, I guess." It was a

canned answer, and one I really didn't mean. I had found it was a sufficient answer to give when people asked why you weren't in a relationship. It was a much better answer than 'I'm too fucked up to be with anyone.'

"Oh, I don't think so. You should meet my son. He's a good one. I raised him well." She smiled wide, intensifying the wrinkles at the corners of her eyes as her entire face seemed to light up. "But I could be biased since I am his momma."

"I didn't realize you had a son. You never mentioned him before." I had always gotten the impression Viv Montgomery was a widow and all alone. She had mentioned once that her husband had passed away many years ago, but that had been the only mention of family.

"I do. He's a handsome boy. He looks like his father did at his age. Thick black hair, hypnotizing brown eyes, firm jawline, muscular build. His Korean blood gives him a rich caramel-colored skin." She giggled. "Can you tell I am a proud mother? Yes, he looks just like his handsome father. My husband always had that powerful hold of my heart. Do you know what I'm talking about? That crazed, all-consuming love you can't live without." She paused, and a look of sadness washed over her face, but then was quickly replaced with a tender smile. "My son reminds me of him so much. Anyway, he's picking me up after my lunch today."

I tilted my head and studied her expression. I saw so much love and pride on her face. But if she truly loved and adored her son so much, why had she not mentioned him before? "I thought you took the bus here and home."

"I used to. But my son told me that, from now on, he would be driving me to the places I needed to go. Such a kind boy."

"Does he live here in town?" I still found it odd Viv had never mentioned him before, and he was just now stepping in to care for her by providing transportation. I couldn't quite silence the warning bells going off in my head.

"Yes. He lives with me for now. He just returned, and it will take him a bit to get on his feet. But I'm in no rush for him to move out. I like having him around."

Ahh, a deadbeat son taking advantage of his mother is what this sounded like.

"What does he do for a living?"

"He's a pilot. He's loved planes from the time he could barely walk."

"You said he just returned. From where?"

Maybe I was being too nosy. But I heard the stories all the time of lazy and greedy family members taking advantage of their elders. I had no knowledge of Viv's financial situation other than the fact that she always paid in cash and would leave a very large tip. Sometimes too large, and she and I would argue about her overpaying me, but she always won out. I hated to think that her own flesh and blood could use her, or that anyone could take advantage of an elder, but I still found it a bit disturbing he was just *now* popping into her life. She had been coming here for months, me feeding her for an hour on those days, and not once did she mention any family at all.

Viv shifted in her seat, appearing uncomfortable. She didn't say anything, but rather opened her mouth to take another bite. I had overstepped it seemed.

"I'm sorry. I didn't mean to... I'm sorry. I'll mind my own business from now on."

Viv finished her bite. "Oh no. I don't mind. It's just hard to answer that question. I always worry he'll be judged and thought poorly of. He's such a decent and fine man, that it's a shame he has this mark on his past." She took a deep breath and continued chewing the food in her mouth.

Feeling guilty for doing exactly that—judging, I said, "Well, I'm the last person who has any business judging people. And we all have marks in our pasts. Some more than others."

Her tiny, frail body leaned inward. Lowering her voice, she asked, "You promise you won't think badly of him? He is such a good man. I would hate for you to think otherwise."

"If you say he is a good man, then I'll believe you." I gave her a reassuring smile. "I can't imagine you raising anyone but a fine, upstanding man anyway."

"He just got out of prison," she blurted, looking terrified the minute she said the words.

The word 'prison' hit too close to home, and I instantly felt sick to my stomach. I didn't want to think of prison. I didn't want to think...

"But he didn't do it!" she said in a hushed, yet aggressive tone. "He would never do the things they said. A man like my son would never kill a girl. They had it all wrong when they said he was guilty."

Prison.

Kill.

Guilty.

I couldn't cope. I couldn't hear these dark words that followed me wherever I went. Not today. Not today!

I put down the fork. "I really need to get to work, Mrs. Montgomery. Maria is covering for me, but she really needs to get home to her baby."

Viv reached out a shaky hand to me. "Oh no. Please tell me I didn't scare you off with the news of my son. Please. I can see I have upset you. He was found guilty of manslaughter, not murder, but I swear to you, he didn't do it. And I feel awful now. I can see you are uncomfortable." She appeared to be broken-hearted, and I had never seen her so upset before.

"It's not that... I have a lot to deal with today." I struggled to hold back the tears threatening to fall. "It's not a very good day for me is all." I took her trembling hand and held it firmly. I wanted to reassure her that my demons were not due to her or the news of her son. My demons only needed the slightest push to be knocking at my door once again.

"I worry you are going to get up from here thinking my son is a bad person." Her lower lip began to quiver. "And he isn't. He really isn't."

I nodded and squeezed her hand again, not wanting my own morose thoughts to upset the woman. "I believe you, Viv. I do. I'm glad you have your son back." And I meant it. I'd always hated the thought of her having to deal with her illness all by herself. Now that her son was home, she wouldn't be alone. I scooted out of the booth and stood. "Bring him in next time, and I'll give him a free piece of Blossoms' famous cherry pie."

Her lip ceased trembling, a warm smile to replace it. "Oh I will. He would love that. You are such a kind girl. He will just adore you."

"Okay, well I really need to get to work," I said. "Are you coming in Tuesday?"

She nodded. "Of course." She clutched her

hands together to her chest. "I can't wait for you two to meet. I promise you will see what a wonderful boy he is. He may be a bit of a momma's boy, but he is such a good, good boy."

One Click the rest of CAPTIVE VOW now.

Made in the USA
Las Vegas, NV
21 September 2021